A GANGSTA
AND HIS
Shawty

Heirs to the Baptiste Throne

A NOVEL BY

NATISHA RAYNOR

Royalty Publishing House is now accepting manuscripts from aspiring or experienced urban romance authors!

WHAT MAY PLACE YOU ABOVE THE REST:

Heroes who are the ultimate book bae: strong-willed, maybe a little rough around the edges but willing to risk it all for the woman he loves.

Heroines who are the ultimate match: the girl next door type, not perfect - has her faults but is still a decent person. One who is willing to risk it all for the man she loves.

The rest is up to you! Just be creative, think out of the box, keep it sexy and intriguing!

If you'd like to join the Royal family, send us the first 15K words (60 pages) of your completed manuscript to submissions@royaltypublishinghouse.com

Synopsis

The Baptiste crew is back with more drama than ever. Jules Jr., better known as J2, is exceptionally smart. He graduated from high school a year early and was accepted into college. No matter how gifted J2 is academically, Baptiste blood runs through his veins, and despite his father's disapproval, he decides that he wants to complete his father's street legacy. No one can juggle running a drug empire and being a college student better than J2. His father always told him that when it comes to hustling, the bad outweighs the good, and J2 begins to see that. When he's not dealing with incompetent, thieving workers, he has to deal with hustlers from out of town trying to infiltrate his blocks. Before he can spring into action, Jules comes to the rescue, making J2 feel some type of way. How can he prove that he's just as good a boss as his father if his father won't let him handle his own business? On top of that, J2 finds himself growing a little too fond of his homegirl Jazlyn, because his heart belongs to Natori.

Jules always forbade Reign from dealing with hustlers, and she always listened. Her father still isn't pleased when she starts dating a rapper by the name of Tre da Don. Jules doesn't trust him as far as he can throw him, but Reign is smitten with the charming man, and soon she's all in. It doesn't take Reign long to realize that her father may have been right about Tre, and for betraying Reign, he may have to pay with his life.

Kymani is unsure about her marriage. She hasn't caught Jacques cheating in ages, but she still has this unsettling feeling. The feeling is nagging her to the point that Kymani takes drastic measures to find out the truth. They say be careful when you go looking for stuff because you just may find it, and she has to learn that the hard way. Kymani and Jacques's relationship will never be the same, but in the end, will the changes be for the better?

Lyric and Jules are still married, and their love is stronger than ever, but Lyric is fighting a demon that no one knows about but her. She understands that she's playing a dangerous game; however, no matter how much she tries to pretend, Lyric no longer has control over her life. This demon is holding her hostage, and she's not even sure that she wants to fight it. When Jules is made aware of the secret, all hell breaks loose, and Lyric is forced to face her problems. The only thing is, she doesn't want to fix her issues. Lyric thinks she's fine, and that puts a strain on her marriage. Jules will never give her up without a fight, but Lyric may need help that even he can't give her.

Chapter One

"Uggggh, I hate when I can't choose," Reign whined into the cell phone that was pressed snugly against her ear. Letting out an exasperated sigh, one would have thought she'd been presented with a truly disheartening task. For a young woman as spoiled as Reign, it was a disheartening task. Having to decide between two expensive designer bags was the epitome of unfair in her world.

"Just get them both, duh," her cousin, Jayla, spoke into the phone, causing Reign to kiss her teeth.

"And have to hear my dad going in about my credit card bill next month? No thanks. Like, what's the point of getting me credit cards if I'm not supposed to use them?" Her whining continued.

"How about I get them both for you?" A deep voice came from behind her.

Reign whirled around to see who was making such an offer, and her eyes had to travel up to land on the person's face. The usually calm, cool, and collected Reign couldn't keep her mouth from falling open in shock. It was Tre da Don standing so close to her that she could reach out and touch him. Tre the muhfuckin' Don! She couldn't believe it. A week ago, Reign spent $900 on a VIP booth in the very club that he was performing in that night. His show was the reason she was in the mall, and this man was in Saks Fifth Avenue offering to buy her not one but two bags.

"Um, Jayla, let me call you back," Reign mumbled into the phone. As the daughter of Jules Baptiste, Reign had the best of everything for as long as she could remember. Spoiled was an understatement. There wasn't a thing on this Earth that she could ever want that Jules couldn't get for her, and for that very reason, Reign usually gave men a hard time. She didn't give a damn who they were. In her mind, nobody exuded more power and wealth than her father, but this man standing before her had her full attention.

Seeing the amused gleam in his eyes, Reign quickly clamped her mouth shut. No matter how stunned she was, the very last thing she would ever do was come across as some starstruck groupie, but gah damn, he was even better looking in person than on Instagram and music videos. Tre da Don stood at six feet even with almond colored skin and tattoos all over his neck and arms. Reign loved thugs; shit, look at who raised her, but she'd still never been too fond of men with tattoos on their faces. However, the small word *Blessed* written in cursive over his left eyebrow was even sexy to her. Between her father and all of her uncles, Reign had been taught the game of life better than some of the most thorough OG's. That being said, she knew enough to know that no man was going to do anything without expecting something in return. Before she fucked for some purses, she'd charge them and just hear Jules's mouth about it.

"And why would you do that?" Reign questioned as the majority of her heightened senses were put to work. After taking in the Versace shirt that hugged his lean frame, inhaling the expensive cologne that smelled rich, and tasting the bitter gloss that she'd licked from her lips, Reign could have sworn that she felt little volts of electricity shooting through her body.

Tre looked over his shoulder at his homeboy and his big, burly security guard. "Y'all niggas go shop or something. Let me breathe. Gah damn." At his command, the men scattered like roaches, and Tre turned his attention back to Reign. Rubbing his hands together as his eyes traveled her body, Tre smirked. Shorty definitely wasn't the average. Even dressed down, he could tell she was of a different caliber.

She wore simple red leggings and a simple red sports bra, but covering her top half was a white, red, and green Gucci jacket, zipped less than halfway. On her feet were Gucci slides, and a matching headband held her long, expensive weave back from her cinnamon colored face. The woman was petite as hell, probably not even a size seven, but she was bad nonetheless. Tre had seen enough fake asses to last a lifetime, so he could appreciate a natural body. On baby girl's wrist was a diamond and platinum Rolex, and from her arm hung an oversized red Gucci hobo bag, but what really made Tre's dick hard was the diamond and gold grills on her bottom teeth. Lil' mama was bad as fuck, and he wanted her in the worst way. Having overheard some of her conversation, he could tell her pops had money. Tre was down for competing with the nigga, whoever he was.

"I just heard a gorgeous young woman trying to decide between two bags, and I decided to help her out. Am I wrong for that?" He licked his lips, and Reign damn near fainted.

"Sooooo, you're willing to spend five thousand dollars on me for two bags? What's the catch, because I don't fuc—"

Tre cut her off. "Whoa, lil' mama, be easy. I'm not asking you for anything. No, scratch that. I am." Reign raised one eyebrow and waited for him to continue. She dared him to say anything disrespectful. "I want you to come to my show tonight. That's it." Every now and then, Tre came across women that weren't impressed by him. Ones that required a little work to get to. He didn't mind the chase if he felt like she was worth it.

Reign decided to play his game just to see how far it would go. In her world, shit like this didn't happen every day. She had met a few celebrities, but this shit was something totally different. "Already done. I have a booth." Reign loved flexin' for niggas. Nothing was funnier than meeting a man that attempted to flaunt his money in an effort to impress her, and she ended up making him look stupid every time. Like the time a dude was in a money throwing competition with her in the strip club. He tapped out after $300 and was embarrassed as fuck when Reign continued to throw money for a good ten minutes after he tapped out.

"Word? What's your name, ma?" Right after the show, Tre was supposed to be heading back to Virginia where he was from. Even with him being who he was, he could already tell the chances of him fucking shorty that night were slim to none, but he was going to make it his business to get to know her.

"Reign."

"Aight, Reign. Get your bags, shorty, so I can pay for them. Can I have your number, or is that too much to ask? I want us to link before I head to the club. You can roll with me."

In her mind, Reign was screaming at the top of her lungs, but on the outside, she looked almost bored. "Cool, we can do that. And thank you."

Tre looked her up and down. "The pleasure is all mine."

Lyric woke up to Jules placing soft kisses along the back of her neck. She giggled and arched her back. "I'm supposed to be sleeping in today." Even after all the years they'd been together, Lyric and Jules still hungered for each other like they'd just met.

Life was different for them. Reign was in her last year of college, and an extremely smart Jules Jr., whom they affectionately called J2, had graduated from high school a year early and was a freshman in college. Their daughter Bella was in middle school and very indepen-dent. Jules had someone running his businesses, so he went to work whenever he wanted. Most of his days were spent researching ways to invest money, working out, shooting hoops, and chilling with his wife and family. He'd put in enough work in the streets. Jules was chilling.

"I know, but I woke up with a hard dick," he mumbled as he kissed her on the shoulder.

"Let's see what we can do about that then." Lyric turned over on her back and smiled as Jules covered her body with his. His bun had come loose, causing his long dreads to drape across his shoulders. Since Lyric didn't sleep with panties on, Jules was inside of her tunnel in no time, and she closed her eyes and moaned.

Lyric opened her legs and bent them back. "Ummmmmm," she moaned as Jules fucked her fast and hard. She loved sex with her husband.

Jules knew Lyric's body as well as he knew his own, so when he knew she was about to cum, he pulled out of her, dipped his head low, and began to eat her out, causing her moans to become louder and louder. Reign lived in an apartment near her college campus, and Jules Jr. had his own apartment as well. Bella was in school, so Lyric was free to scream bloody murder as her husband sucked her essence from her body.

"Shit, baby. Oh my God, yes!" she whimpered as her body shook.

With a grin, Jules came up for air and plunged back into Lyric's juicy middle with a grunt. One of his fears of marriage was becoming bored with the same person, but he would never tire of Lyric's gushy greatness. It was if her pussy was made just for him. Placing one of her legs over his shoulder, he hit her with a stroke so deep, she felt it in her stomach. "Where you want this shit, baby?" Jules growled, referring to his semen.

Lyric didn't answer verbally; instead, she opened her mouth and stuck her tongue out, turning him on even more. "Fuck." He hissed as he pulled out of her once again.

Sitting up, Lyric took him into her mouth and sucked his dick hungrily. In less than a minute, his seeds were shooting down her throat, and he was growling like a bear. This was how he loved to start his day. After he and Lyric took a shower together, they brushed their teeth and got dressed for the day. She knew that Jules was about to have his morning blunt, so she headed downstairs to cook him breakfast and get a morning kick of her own as well.

Years of doing hair gave Lyric terrible cramps and spasms in her fingers and hands. She still had her salon, but she only did hair a few times a month. Lyric truly missed doing hair, and when she had to stop working full-time, the first few months were really hard on her. The children were older and didn't need her as much, and Lyric felt like she had no purpose. Being that some days the cramps were bad enough to almost bring her to tears, the doctor prescribed her some pretty strong pain medication. It wasn't really that serious, but Lyric had been coming to her for years, and the women had a slight friendship. Seeing it as a favor to her to give her the "good stuff," the doctor gave her sixty Percocets.

Being depressed and bored had Lyric taking the pills even on the days her fingers didn't cramp or spasm. She saw no harm in what she was doing, not knowing the dependency that her body was starting to have for the pills. It was nine months later, and Lyric was still popping pills every day, several times a day. No one knew. It was Lyric's little secret. All she had to do was go to her doctor, summon a few tears, and talk about how she wished the pain would just end, and boom, she'd have another prescription. Once Jules was busy rolling his blunt, Lyric grabbed a juice from the fridge and threw the pill she was holding into her mouth. Percs were now the only way she could start her day.

Chapter Two

"Don't forget, your papers are due Monday!" the professor yelled out as thirty students stood up from their seats and gathered their belongings to leave her class.

J2 stood up with his backpack in hand. After shoving his calculus book, laptop, and folder inside, he headed to the door where his home-girl Jazlyn was waiting for him.

"Bye, Jules," a girl sang out. He didn't even know her name, but he tipped his head in her direction. Money, his father's street fame, and his swagged out demeanor, got him the attention of many. It had been that way his entire life, and he was pretty much used to it.

There wasn't a man breathing that J2 admired more than his father. They had the same honey colored skin tone, and even the same long dreads. Lyric twisted Jules Jr.'s hair when he was three, and he'd been growing locs ever since. Him being younger than everyone in the class, was something that only he and Jazlyn knew. Because of who his father was, J2 was always mature. He was quiet, and people watched a lot. He had the demeanor of a thirty-year-old man rather than one that was barely eighteen. As soon as he neared Jazlyn, she started walking through the door, causing J2 to nudge her.

"I see you on that quiet shit today, huh?" him and Jazlyn clicked so much because she was just like him. What some people considered to be moody, was just how Jazlyn and J2 were. Some days, they weren't in the mood to talk, and most people didn't understand that.

Because of the fact that she shut down often, her friends and associates wrote her off as being bipolar. Jazlyn hated that people didn't respect her wishes to some days just want to be left alone, but J2 got it. They had been friends ever since they were paired together for an exercise during freshman orientation. Jazlyn was gorgeous. With dark skin and almond shaped eyes, she looked like a doll, but J2 didn't try to get at her on that level. He saw something in her that he clicked with. There was a sadness in her eyes that she often tried to hide, but J2 could notice it when no one else did. He didn't press her about what was wrong. He just did what a friend does, and he was always there for her, even if that meant simply being quiet with her.

Jazlyn smiled. "Shut up. What you about to do? Want to grab some food before you head back to your apartment while us lowly peasants retreat to the dorm?" she joked.

J2's girlfriend, Natori didn't like him hanging with Jazlyn, and for that reason, he kept their friendship on the low. Natori didn't attend North Carolina Central University with them, so he was free to do what he pleased without hearing her mouth.

"Yeah, we can do that. I bet you want to stop by that wing spot, huh? Yo' ass gon' turn into a chicken." He chuckled as they headed for his chocolate Range Rover.

"Chicken makes me happy." Jazlyn smiled, and a rare sparkle gleamed in her eyes.

J2 smiled. He loved it when Jazlyn was truly happy, because it never seemed to last long. "Aight then. Let's go. I'll buy you a twelve piece today, just 'cause I'm that nigga."

Jazlyn laughed, and the friends climbed inside his truck.

An hour and a half later, J2 rolled up in one of the hoods on Durham's south side. He parked in front of a run-down blue house and sat patiently waiting for Kareem to come out. Half a minute after he pulled up, Kareem jogged down the porch steps with a backpack on his back. "What's good, boss?" he asked as he sat the book bag on the floor of the Range and unzipped it, allowing J2 to peek inside.

With his hand resting lightly on the gun that sat in his lap, J2 sat up a bit and peered at the stacks of cash. "Count that shit," he demanded, grabbing a money counting machine from the back seat.

J2 lit a blunt and watched intently as Kareem fed the machine stack after stack. Minutes later, when J2 saw that his trap house's total take was exactly what it should be and not a dollar less, he nodded his head. "Aight. Y'all good in there?"

"Yep. Won't need to re-up 'til tomorrow afternoon sometime."

"Aight. J.J. will be here in the morning to get you straight." J.J. was Jacques' son and J2's first cousin.

"Bet." Kareem exited the truck and headed back inside the house.

J2 pulled off. His next stop was his trap on the north side of Raleigh. Everything J2 did, he did well. His parents sent him to the best schools. He was naturally smart and adapted well. When he graduated a year early with a 4.0 GPA, Jules gifted him with a brand-new, fully-loaded Range. After he was accepted into Central, Jules gave him access to the bank account that he'd been putting money into since J2 was born. With that money, J2 would have been straight until he graduated from college, but no matter how sheltered from the streets Jules kept him, that street shit was in J2's veins.

Many would call him stupid, but he didn't want to just be some spoon-fed rich kid. He challenged himself to be half the man his father was, and J2 wanted to leave behind his own legacy. His father damn near had a fit when J2 told him he wanted to hustle for a few years and turn his inheritance into a few mil. It was his personal goal to graduate from college a millionaire. Jules didn't understand after all he'd sacrificed for him, why his son wanted to live that life. It came with way more bad than good, but J2 was determined.

Just as Jules' father couldn't talk him out of the streets, he couldn't talk J2 out of it. Jules tried to ignore it for months. Initially, he decided to let J2 fall flat on his face, but his heart wouldn't allow that. His son had a better chance at success if Jules guided him and taught him the way. He forbade J2 from being a lowly corner boy. He suggested that J2 get a trustworthy crew to get off the work for him. He spent hours upon hours teaching his son the game, and with a heavy heart, he watched his son become the heir to the Baptiste street throne.

"About time you got here." Natori smiled at J2 as he entered his upscale downtown condo. He and Natori didn't live together, but she had a key to his place. Natori was a year older than him and had bypassed college to do hair. She was actually a stylist in his mother's shop. "I cooked." She smiled, getting up off the couch and walking over to him.

"I just ate. I'll eat it later." He kissed her on the lips and palmed her fat ass.

"We still going to see Tre da Don tonight? You know how you like to flake on me and tell me to just go with my friends."

J2 sat down on the couch and flicked the tip of his nose. "I never flake on you without good reason. As long as nothing comes up, I'm in there."

"Let's go to the mall. I need something to wear."

"Can't." J2 kicked off his Gucci sneakers. "I have to work on this paper that's due Monday. You can go though. Here." He pulled some money from his pocket.

Natori shook her head. It amazed her that her smart, educated, man was a college student and king of the streets. She sighed. "I wanted us to go together, but okay. I'll go and let you get to work because tonight, I need you to be all mine. Got that?" She leaned down and pecked him on the lips.

"I got you, baby."

J2 eased out of the apartment while Natori was in the shower preparing for the night. If she knew he was leaving, she'd start bitching, but he wasn't going to flake on her. Jazlyn hit him up at the last minute wanting to use his laptop, and he told her he'd be there. His paper was done, and he had two MacBooks, plus a PC. He chose not to live too far from campus to lessen the amount of days he was late to class, so he was only about fifteen minutes from Jazlyn. He would be home in plenty enough time to take a shower and make it to the club. Clubs didn't start jumping until around midnight anyway. He'd been to Jazlyn's dorm room a few times, so he knew exactly where to go.

Once he arrived at her room door, J2 tapped on the door twice with his knuckle. The door opened slightly when he knocked, and he peeked his head in, in search of Jazlyn. He didn't see her, so he stepped into the room. Deciding that maybe she stepped out, he placed the laptop on her bed and pulled his phone from his pocket to text her. Suddenly, the bathroom door opened, and she stepped out dressed in only a tank top that he could see through and her big, chocolate nipples made his dick jump. Black panties were the only thing covering her bottom half. Upon seeing J2 standing in her room, she let out a yelp and tried to cover her crotch area with her hands.

"Sorry, the door was open," he said sheepishly, grabbing her robe from her bed and passing it to her.

As she reached out to grab it, he couldn't help but to notice the marks on her thighs. He assumed they rarely saw the sun because her legs were lighter than her face and arms. Just light enough for him to see the remnants of scars. They looked like small burn marks. The scars were round, like maybe they'd been done with a cigarette. When Jazlyn saw him looking at her legs, she threw the robe on and closed it. Since it wasn't long enough to cover the marks, she quickly turned her back and headed to her dresser to get some sweats.

"Um, it's okay. Thank you for bringing the laptop." Her words came out fast and anxious.

J2 noticed marks on the back of her thighs as well. Either Jazlyn was clumsy as hell, or she was the type to self-harm. Unless, maybe someone else did it when she was younger. He wanted to ask, but he wasn't sure if he should. After slipping on the sweats that she pulled from the drawer, Jazlyn turned around to face him, but her gaze was on the floor rather than his face. "You good?" he asked voice full of concern.

Jazlyn looked up at her friend and gave him a fake, tense smile. "I'm great. I will do all of my homework and return your laptop to you Monday."

"No rush. I have another one at home. I'll let you get to work." He slipped out of the room deciding that when she was ready to talk to him, she would. At least he hoped so.

Tears burned Jazlyn's eyes as she looked at the closed door that J2 had just slipped through. She usually had a lie prepared for doctors or anyone else that came across her old burns, but his presence caught her so off guard, and since he technically didn't mention them, she didn't know what to say. Jazlyn sat down on the bed praying that he'd just forget what he saw and never bring it up. Jazlyn had become accustomed to avoiding looking at that part of her body as much as she could. Every time her gaze fell on the marks, she was reminded of her ugly past. Those burns played a major part in her checking out some days and not having much to say.

Her pain ran deep, and some days, she just couldn't smile through her sadness. She couldn't forget, and she couldn't understand why she suffered some of the things that she did. Not even leaving home and coming to college helped her to escape the depression that was buried deep within her. Aside from depression, Jazlyn found it hard to trust people. She knew that she could trust J2 and depend on him, and yet she still only let him in so much. Jazlyn didn't want to be judged, and she didn't want people to feel pity for her. She also wanted to avoid being vulnerable around him. When his sexy, super smart, rich looking ass befriended her, neither Jazlyn or any of the other girls around campus could believe it. She was a pretty girl, but she didn't fit the expectations of who they thought he would be with. Jazlyn was nothing like Natori. When she saw that he really did just want to just be her friend, and he didn't want anything from her, she was relieved a little. But it lowkey made her sad because Jazlyn was deeply in love with J2, but obviously he damn sure didn't feel the same. He friend zoned her from the day they met, and she knew that's where she would more than likely stay, so she kept her desire for him to herself.

Chapter Three

"You smoke?" Tre asked Reign as he held out a fat ass blunt.

"Yeah," she replied coolly taking the blunt from him.

Her dad smoked weed like a chain smoker smokes cigarettes, so she had been around it her entire life. Reign wasn't a pothead like her dad, but one joint a day usually got her right. For as cool as she was trying to seem, she was in awe that her and her cousin, Jayla were on a tour bus with Tre da Don. To make the situation even crazier, Reign was snapping her and Jayla while trying to leave him and his crew out of the short videos. She didn't want Tre to think she was trying to blast him or put him out there, but to her surprise, he hopped in one of her snaps, and that blew her ass away. Tre da Don was on her Snapchat! After that, her DM's started blowing up crazy. Reign had always been popular, and she'd been getting attention her entire life, but this shit was on another level. Word got around fast as hell because an hour after she posted the snap, she had sixty new followers.

Tre snuggled up close to her so he could speak directly in her ear. "So am I going to be able to see you again after tonight, or is this it?" His deep baritone voice in her ear, made a chill run down her spine. Even though in her eyes, she was 'that bitch' Reign didn't know what this twenty-nine-year-old rapper with two children wanted with her. She was still in college and barely old enough to drink legally. She was no longer a teenager, but there was no denying that this man was way more experienced in life than she was. And for as fine as he was, Reign wasn't sure she was ready to be running behind a rapper, playing step-mother to his kids and shit. Hell nah. That would be too much.

"I don't know. Aren't you busy traveling?" She turned to face him as she blew weed smoke through her nostrils.

"Yeah. I'll be in Virginia for two days, and then I go to Atlanta, Jersey, and Miami. Maybe I could fly you out, and you could chill with me for a day or two," he suggested as he eyed her pretty ass thighs.

Reign was dressed in short white shorts, a white bodysuit top with a slit cut in the front, showcasing the sides of her small B cup breasts and pierced belly button, and on her feet were black Yves Saint Laurent heels. She matched his fly in her Rolex, a diamond tennis bracelet, two gold necklaces, and her grills were still in her mouth. Tre wanted shorty so bad he was willing to do whatever to get her.

"I don't know," Reign replied skeptically before biting the inside of her jaw. "I'm in college, and my parents don't play that missing class shit. I would only be able to fly out on the weekends."

Tre's eyes roamed back up to her face. "I can dig it. So, Friday, I have to go to Miami. What if I fly you out Friday and you stay with me until Sunday?"

Reign hit the blunt and passed it to Jayla. "What do you want from me, Tre? I know good and well you have women throwing themselves at you day and night. Why me? Someone that's in school and that won't have the time to spare like that."

Tre respected her being in school, but no way would she still want to put school before him once she got to know him. Yeah, her daddy spoiled her and all that, but he could give her something her daddy couldn't. That dick. Once Tre had Reign where he wanted her, she'd go from being a daddy's girl to his girl. He didn't give a damn about the plethora of groupies that he had, he wanted her ass. "Damn, a nigga can't want you? You fly as fuck. You're beautiful, and I like you. The fact that you're in school is a plus. Most of the women that throw themselves at me just want to be saved. I can tell you got your own."

Reign gave him a subtle smile. The weed had her feeling good, and he'd given her a good answer. Still, she didn't know him well enough to promise him that she'd fly to Miami next weekend. "I'll see. And I don't go anywhere dolo. I don't know you like that, so if I go, my cousin Jayla has to come."

"You ain't said nothing but a word," Tre stated as the tour bus pulled up to the club.

Being that it was after midnight, the club was already packed. Reign's heart felt like it did a cartwheel in her chest as he stood up and grabbed her hand. Leading her off the bus, she wondered if her blushing was visible to those looking at her. Two huge security guards led Tre through the crowded club with him holding on tightly to Reign's hand. Her other hand was behind her, and Jayla held tightly onto it. Reign didn't want to get separated from her cousin. She had already given a few of her homegirls the okay to use her booth, since her and Jayla were with Tre. As he maneuvered through the crowd up to his own VIP section near the stage, Reign heard all of the females screaming and she had to look down because of all of the flashes and lights from cell phones were blinding. She wondered if she would end up on the blogs, and she hoped that she wouldn't.

Reign liked the attention from Tre, but she wasn't all that excited to be in the spotlight when it came to the world. Being the star of Raleigh, North Carolina was cool. Anyone that knew who Jules was, showed Reign nothing but respect no matter where she went. She really was good in any hood, but she had no need to play those kinds of places. When she was younger, being in the projects around all of the action excited her. It was far more interesting than her quiet, bougie neighborhood, but after Jules came and dragged her back to her side of town every time, she stopped going. Though he was retired, Reign had no interest in her or her family's dirt and past being drudged up once people wanted to know who the girl on Tre's arm was.

Reign's phone was going off so much that her battery was almost dead, but the texts she refused to ignore were those of her protectors, J2 and J.J. They saw her come in and of course her brother hit her up wondering what she was doing with Tre da Don. Reign was older than J2, but try telling him that and be hit with a glare that would intimidate Satan himself. J2 had been raised to always protect his sisters, his cousins, and any other female that he cared about. After giving J2 a brief rundown of how she met Tre in the mall and assuring him that she wasn't on any groupie shit, Reign put her phone away and watched with a smile as Tre rocked the crowd. Reign felt a million emotions all at once. She was proud, she was nervous, and she was flattered. What if Tre was really interested in her? What would she do?

"Are you sure you want to do this?" The older woman looked at Kymani with a face full of concern. The elder voodoo priestess usually made it a point not to care what her clients did. It was her duty to warn them of possible dangers that came along with opening certain doors, but once she gave her disclaimer, she didn't care too much if they took heed to her warnings or not.

This woman seemed very troubled however, and something about her had Beline concerned. Women coming in about their man was nothing new to her, but this woman, there was something different about her. There was a shadow of sadness surrounding her. Beline didn't have to be gifted to sense it, and what couldn't be felt could be seen. The look in Kymani's eyes made it obvious that if she found out anything other than what she wanted to hear, it would cause her a great deal of pain. Still, Beline had a job to do.

"Yes, I'm sure." The way that Kymani fidgeted in her seat, represented the exact opposite of the words coming out of her mouth, but Beline decided not to challenge her.

In her wrinkled, brown hand was a tiny vial of red liquid. Beline extended her arm and handed Kymani the concoction. "Put this in his food or drink. Wait ten minutes, then ask him what it is that you would like to know," she instructed.

Kymani took the potion, and a sense of relief washed over her. It would seem crazy to most that she was relying on voodoo to get answers from her husband, but desperate times called for desperate measures. Even though it had been years since Kymani found out about Jacques cheating with Rella, she still couldn't get over the insecurity that came along with being cheated on by someone that you love. Kymani was a beautiful woman, and she ignored advances from men every day. It also seemed that with every advance that she ignored, something in her marriage changed. She and Jacques were nowhere near as close as they used to be. These days, it seemed as if they were just existing, and after raising three kids with him, with only one being biologically hers, Kymani was ready to know if she should keep fighting or just move on. If he didn't love her the same, and he needed to be with multiple women to be happy, then she would kindly remove herself from the equation.

"Thank you." Kymani paid for her item and anxiously left the shop. The way the woman was looking at her was lowkey freaking her out.

As uncertain as she may have appeared or as fragile as others always seemed to think that she was, Kymani didn't want to be pitied. She was tired of coming across as that weak and naïve woman. She loved Jacques, but it seemed as if overnight she had gained strength out of nowhere, and if her marriage wasn't meant to be, then she could walk away easier than she would have been able to do years ago. Her daughter with Jacques, Arianna was in middle school. J.J. and Jayla were out of school and doing their own thing. J.J. took after his father and was in the streets, and Jayla went to Central with Reign. The girls were actually roommates. J.J.'s mother died giving birth to him, and Jayla's mother India was a deadbeat that tested Jacques' gangsta one too many times, so she was no longer among the living either. Jacques spoiled all of his kids, and Kymani raised and loved them just the same. No one would ever be able to guess which kids weren't hers by the way they were treated. Kymani didn't play that favoritism shit.

When she arrived at the large five-bedroom home that she shared with Jacques and Arianna, Kymani went into the kitchen to prepare dinner. She didn't want to have to prepare two separate meals, so she figured her best bet would be to put the potion in Jacques' drink. Some people didn't believe in voodoo, but Kymani had been married to a Haitian long enough to know that it was very real. She just hoped that the woman she went to wasn't a fraud. As a nurse, Kymani often worked long, demanding hours, but she had two days off. Using that opportunity to clean the house from top to bottom and take care of her family, Kymani also prepared a small feast that was sure to last a few days. Ten minutes after the Cajun salmon, grilled shrimp, lobster tails, pasta salad, wild rice, and steaks were done, Arianna walked through the door. Not wanting to eat without Jacques, Kymani passed time by talking to her daughter about her day at school and asking her how cheerleading practice went.

"Can we go ahead and eat without dad? I'm starving," Arianna begged.

Seeing movement from her peripheral vision, Kymani looked out of the front window and saw Jacques pulling up in his Rolls Royce. "He's here. Go wash your hands, and I'll fix your plate."

Kymani's heart beat like a drum in her chest as she stood up and headed for the kitchen. After quickly swiping the vial of liquid from her purse, Kymani moved swiftly to fix Jacques a glass of Hennessy. He had the same routine. Multiple blunts a day and at least two glasses of cognac before bed. Kymani was so nervous that her hands trembled, as she dropped a few ice cubes into a glass and grabbed a bottle of liquor. Hearing the alarm chirp on his car and the water no longer running in the downstairs bathroom, Kymani popped open the vial and poured the liquid into the glass. It wasn't even enough to cover the entire bottom of the glass, so Kymani prayed he wouldn't taste it. She shoved the empty vial into her back pocket and opened the bottle of Henny just as the front door opened and Arianna greeted her father.

Kymani poured a double shot of liquor and picked the glass up to swirl the liquor around. She'd just grabbed two plates when Jacques walked his tall, lanky, sexy ass in the kitchen with his daughter at his side, and his arm draped around her shoulder. No matter how many times he wasn't a good husband, Jacques had always been a good father, and his children adored him. Kymani gave him a smile as she handed him the glass of liquor. "Hi, I was just about to fix your plate."

Jacques' dreads touched the middle of his back and he was clad in light denim jeans, a plain white tee, and white Louboutin sneakers. On his wrist was a rose gold Rolex and from his neck hung a long platinum chain with a diamond encrusted B. His platinum wedding band completed his jewelry. Even with an eye missing from being shot, Jacques was one of the sexiest men that Kymani had ever lay her eyes on.

"Thanks." Jacques took the glass, and Kymani fixed all of their plates.

It took them well over ten minutes to eat, so Kymani hoped that by the time she began to question him, that the truth would be the only thing to come out of his mouth. She rehearsed what she wanted to ask him over and over in her mind. Finally, Arianna retreated to her room, and Jacques stood to pour himself another shot of liquor.

Blowing out a shaky breath, Kymani looked over at Jacques and tried to calm her nerves. "Can I ask you something?" she asked in a soft voice.

"What's up?"

"Are you happy in this marriage?" As soon as the words left her mouth, Kymani waited with baited breath for Jacques to answer. Lord knows, it would hurt her if he said anything other than yes, but she needed to know. She also hoped that she wouldn't regret delving into the religion or the practice of voodoo. Being raised in a Christian family, she'd always been advised against such things and taught that it was wrong.

Jacques' eyebrows furrowed. He and Kymani hadn't beefed in weeks, and they'd just made love last night. He hated these kinds of questions, and he hated when she wanted to have these long deep talks. He hadn't done shit, and he was tired of defending himself. What was even more strange to him was the fact that he wanted to say yes. He fixed his mouth to say yes, but that's not what came out. "Some days."

Immediately, he saw Kymani's face fall, and he wanted to kick his own ass for not telling her what she needed to hear. What she wanted to hear. Maybe his subconscious was tired of lying and putting up a front. Either way, he could tell by the solemn look on her face that he was probably in for a night of dramatics. Needing the liquid courage, Jacques took a big gulp of his drink.

"What do you mean some days?"

"Kymani, I haven't cheated on you in a long ass time. Like a long time, but you question me, and go through my phone, and give me hell at least once a month. I'm tired of the shit. Like I've said a million times before, I'm the reason that you're insecure, but it's been years. Forgive me and move on from it, or just don't." Jacques wasn't sure how a nice peaceful, delicious dinner, had turned into this. An argument just lurking in the shadows waiting to explode. Letting out a frustrated sigh, he drained his glass and poured another drink.

Kymani's mouth fell open from shock, but this was what she asked for. It was what she paid for, and she wasn't going to stop questioning him until she knew everything that she needed to know. "When is the last time you cheated on me?" she asked in a determined voice. Kymani didn't even let the dark cloud that covered Jacques' good eye deter her. He was getting angry, but she didn't care.

"I'm not doing this with you." He turned to walk away, leaving her in the kitchen.

Kymani knew that if she continued to badger him and ask him questions that he didn't want to answer, that Jacques would blow up, but she had to keep going. She followed him into the living room where he pulled a sack of weed from his pocket and grabbed his cigars from behind a picture on the bookshelf. Jacques had cigars stashed in every room of the house. Standing in front of the couch with her arms folded underneath her breasts, Kymani eyed him as he sat down. She wasn't letting up.

Jacques let out an angry chuckle. "After you found out about me and Rella. I told you I deaded shit, but I fucked her a few more times after that. You never found out." He didn't even give her the respect of eye contact as he split his cigar. "That was the last time. Years ago. Now, what the fuck you gon' do with that information?" he asked boldly.

Kymani was stunned to say the least. She watched him roll his blunt not sure if she wanted to slap the shit out of him or continue to pry. Indeed, it had been a very long time since he cheated on her with Rella. So, did she appreciate the fact that he hadn't cheated on her in years, or did she become furious that after she took him back and he promised that he was done with Rella, he fucked her again. Kymani was torn, and it wasn't an answer that she would be able to come up with in a matter of seconds. He hadn't done anything recently, so maybe she should have left well enough alone. Fuck! All of her uncertainty and doubt left when Jacques finally looked up with that cold glare in his eye and a smirk on his caramel colored face. It was as if he was silently daring her to do something. Angry tears burned her eyes.

"You ain't shit." Was all that she could get out.

Jacques pulled a lighter from his pocket, while never breaking eye contact with Kymani. "I know I fucked up. I fucked up quite a few times, and you forgave me. Even after you forgave me, I still went and fucked up some more, and I was dead ass wrong for that. That's why all these years that I haven't touched another bitch, I put up with all ya shit. The going through my phone, the accusations. It was my fault for placing that doubt in your head, and I took my punishment like a man. Even when I was mad at you and not even sure I wanted to be married to you anymore, I still haven't touched another woman. It been fuckin' years, Kymani. All the questioning, the going through my shit, it all ends today, or this marriage ends. You got that?" he asked just before clenching his jaw muscles.

Rage consumed Kymani. She prayed that Arianna had her headphones in, because what she wanted to get off her chest, were words that she refused to say in an inside voice. "You have no fucking right to threaten to end this marriage because you're tired of me questioning you. You've made it clear to me numerous times that you didn't deserve my trust. I let you back in our home, and you slept with her again?" Tears spilled over Kymani's eyelids. Even if the infidelity had been committed years ago, it still hurt. Even after she found out about Rella, Jacques still wouldn't cut her off, so it had to be about more than sex.

'Even when I was mad at you and not even sure I wanted to be married to you anymore, I still haven't touched another woman.' Those words played over in her mind. So there were times that he was unhappy and wanted out. No marriage was perfect. All couples had their ups and downs, so why were there times that he didn't want to be married to her anymore? Had she failed as a wife? Even after she raised kids that weren't hers and never complained once. She was faithful to him even after he wasn't faithful to her, and there were still times that he didn't want her? Kymani's feelings were beyond hurt.

"I'm not doing this shit with you right now. If you want to be mad and cry about some shit that's more than five years old, then you be my muhfuckin' guest, but get the fuck up out my face with the shit," he stated coolly as he puffed from his blunt.

Jacques could be one of the sweetest men on this Earth, or he could be a cold, callous, disrespectful son of a bitch. It was rare that he turned up on Kymani, but she could see it in his eyes, that this would be the night if she didn't leave well enough alone. She just stared at him unsure of what to do. Since there seemed to be times when he didn't want to be married, she had half a mind to pack her shit and leave. After three kids, numerous years, two homes, blood, sweat, and tears, could she really pack her shit and walk away? Just as Kymani was about to retreat to their bedroom, a ghastly look covered Jacques' face.

He looked up at her with a confused look on his face, before jumping up with blunt still in hand, and fleeing to the bathroom. Kymani's eyes widened in shock as she listened to him puke up all the food that he'd eaten at dinner. Fear swelled in her gut and caused beads of sweat to decorate her forehead. What if Beline had given her some kind of poison? What if it killed Jacques? What the fuck had she done? It had to be what she'd given him. Kymani had seen her husband polish off a pint of liquor in one night with no trace of a hangover the next day. He'd hadn't drunk nearly enough liquor to be throwing up. In the entire time that they'd been together, she saw him throw up once. Years ago, when he had the stomach flu. Kymani stood in the middle of their living room too scared to go after him.

Jacques rinsed his mouth out and looked at his reflection in the mirror as his stomach churned. After staring at himself for more than a minute, his face began to distort like something off of a horror movie. "The fuck?" He jumped back chest heaving up and down.

What in the fuck was going on with him? After he moved, his face went back to normal, but the image was stuck in his head. He was nowhere near drunk. A little buzz damn sure wouldn't have him seeing shit. He wasn't smoking a new batch of weed, so what was good? Thinking hard as hell, he remembered how Kymani had been the one to hand him his drink. He remembered how every question she asked him, he'd been compelled to tell the truth, even when he knew she wouldn't like the answer. Jacques wasn't new to that shit. His aunt Vi had been doing it for his entire life. Storming out of the bathroom, he stalked over to the couch and grabbed his cellphone with a deep scowl etched on his face. Kymani was still glued to the same spot, looking crazy as hell. Jacques' guts bubbled as he waited anxiously for his aunt to answer. As soon as she did, he barked into the phone.

"How can I know if a bitch put some shit on me?"

Kymani gasped. How in the hell did he know? As she watched him pace back and forth while listening intently, fear gripped her like a vice. She listened to Jacques recant how he drank something that she'd given him. Then he started answering all of her questions truthfully, right before throwing up, and his guts were bubbling. Before he could finish talking on the phone, he went into the bathroom and shut the door behind him. Kymani dropped down onto the couch with more tears pooling in her eyes. She'd fucked up big time. Had she just left well enough alone, they wouldn't be where they were at this very moment. The tables had turned fast as hell, and now Kymani sat afraid like hell of the outcome.

Time seemed to move slow as hell. She heard his muffled voice from the bathroom as he talked to his aunt. When Jacques finally emerged from the bathroom, he was no longer on the phone and rage danced in his eyes. He came and took her previous spot, so that he was now standing in front of her. "What did you give me? It won't do you any good to lie because I'm catching a flight in the morning. Whatever you put on me, my aunt gon' take that shit right back off." He seethed.

Kymani looked up at him and wrung her hands nervously. It really would do her no good to lie. Vi was the real deal. "I didn't put anything *on* you. It was a truth serum. I just wanted to know if you were still cheating on me." Her voice cracked.

Jacques scoffed. "This is some straight up bullshit, and you know it. Well, now you got the truth, and I hope it made you happy. I'm done with this shit, yo. I don't want to be married. You can keep the crib. I'm out."

All Kymani could do was sob as Jacques turned and headed up the stairs. What had she done?

Chapter Four

J2 spotted Jazlyn as he headed across the campus to his next class. He only took three classes a day Monday through Thursday, and two classes on Friday. He neared her, wondering what type of mood she was in, as he heard a short dark-skinned guy calling out to her. It was obvious by the way she rolled her eyes upwards that Jazlyn heard him, she just elected not to turn around and acknowledge him.

"Fuck you then, bitch," the guy barked as his two homeboys laughed.

J2 had no doubt inherited his father's temper, and anger coursed through his body as he walked right past a confused Jazlyn and over to the group of guys. The loud, boisterous one noticed J2 right away. Everyone on campus knew who the man was, and he was shocked, but pleased that the man was in his presence. J2 was dressed in Balmain and had sneakers on his feet that cost a car payment. He was indeed the man, and the disrespectful guy forgot all about Jazlyn. "What up, lil' Jules?" He held out his hand for dap. Some people called him Lil' Jules, and J2 didn't oppose to it. He was honored to be the son of the infamous Jules Baptiste, but the man that stood before him wasn't a friend of his. Before anyone could blink, J2 rocked off on dude, hitting him so hard that spit flew from his mouth.

J2 looked over his shoulder at a confused Jazlyn as the guy that he hit stumbled back a few feet, dazed and bewildered as to why he'd been hit. J2 jerked his head, motioning Jazlyn to come over to him. He could see the hesitancy on her face as a small crowd gathered. J2 didn't give a damn who was looking. He was big on respect, and anybody that he cared about would never be disrespected in his presence without consequences.

As the young man held his bloody mouth, he was no doubt embarrassed, but he knew better than to try J2. Dying wasn't something that he was ready to do. "What the fuck is good?" he asked, not even bothering to try and fight back.

"You called my homie a bitch. I think you need to apologize to the lady." J2 seethed.

"It's not that serious, really," Jazlyn stated, touching J2's arm in an effort to put out the fire that was dancing in his eyes. She appreciated him taking up for her, but the manner in which he was doing it made her uneasy. Her eyes darted around the growing crowd, and it was making her uncomfortable.

"Yes, the fuck it is that serious," J2 growled, never taking his eyes off old boy.

"I'm sorry. I didn't mean anything by it." He groveled as blood seeped through his fingers. "I'm sorry," he repeated, his gaze shifting over to Jazlyn.

Satisfied with the apology, J2 turned and headed for his class, and Jazlyn followed. "Jules Baptiste Junior, that is not acceptable behavior on a college campus," she chastised. Though she felt honored, she didn't want him to get in trouble on her account.

"Fuck all that you talking about. Muhfuckas gon' respect you in my presence," J2 challenged adamantly.

Jazlyn headed to her class with mixed feelings. She almost wished that J2 looked at her as more than a friend, but she also knew that with as damaged and inexperienced as she was, she wouldn't even know what to do with a man like that.

"Can you tell me why you knocked some nigga out today at school over that Jazlyn broad?" Natori asked as she burst into J2's apartment later that night. She'd been stuck in the salon doing hair until 9 p.m. but as soon as she was done, she headed for her man's place ready to question him about the latest gossip.

J2 flipped his biology book closed. "I didn't knock nobody out. Muhfuckas stay exaggerating. I rocked a nigga though for calling my people a bitch. What's it to you?" he asked as he stared her down.

"What's it to me?" Natori raised an eyebrow. "It looks like *my* nigga is fighting over the next broad. That's what it is to me. If I had a male friend, you wouldn't be having that shit. I need you to tone down whatever it is that you got going on with this bitch." Natori snaked her neck. "You really risked being put out of school to play Captain Save a Hoe?"

J2 began to feverishly twist one of his locs in his hand, a habit that he picked up from his father. He did it when he was bored, mad, or nervous. "You don't tell me what the fuck to do," he stated in a calm voice. "Shorty is my friend. I have never done anything even slightly inappropriate with her. If you can't accept that, then I don't know what the fuck to tell you. He was disrespectful, and I handled that shit. Chill the fuck out."

Natori scoffed. She didn't like the attachment that her man had to another female. She tried to be cool with it, but she just wasn't feeling it. "Do you like her?" she blurted, out not even trying to hide her insecurity.

Bored with the conversation, J2 stood up and walked up on Natori. "Who am I with every fucking day and night? Am I with her or you?" He gritted, staring her down.

Despite how angry she'd previously been, Natori's clit thumped as her man hit her with the death glare. She loved J2's aggressive, thugged out ass. She still didn't like him being friends with another female, but when daddy laid down the law, it made her pussy cream something terrible. Rather than speaking, Natori placed a soft kiss on his lips. J2 picked her up, and with her legs wrapped around his waist, he carried her to the bedroom. Not in the mood for gentle lovemaking, J2 dropped her on the bed, causing her body to bounce off the $3,000 mattress. Natori lay there mesmerized as J2 looked her in the eyes while undressing.

Once his Versace boxer briefs were off, and his caramel colored dick stood at attention, Natori was snapped back to the present as she slid off her jeans and panties. J2 covered her body with his and entered her forcefully causing her to moan. "Oh my God, baby," she whined as he fucked her hard and fast.

He wasn't in the mood for her mouth, and he fucked her with aggression to lead her thoughts elsewhere. It worked, because less than ten minutes in, Natori was having an orgasm and apologizing to her man. "I'm so sorry, baby. Ohhhhh, I love you so much," she cried out as her pussy muscles contracted on his dick.

Ignoring her words, J2 plowed into her harder and deeper. It was crazy as hell to him that he'd never thought about Jazlyn in that way until Natori mentioned it. When she asked him if he liked her, he wasn't sure what his honest to God answer would have been. He truly did like her as a friend, but was that it? J2 didn't like being unsure, so to distract himself, he fucked the shit out of his girlfriend, until she was screaming out his name and crying real tears. Even after he busted a fat nut, and Natori had calmed all the way down, the question still ate at him. Did he like Jazlyn as more than a friend?

"Jules!" Lyric's eyes darted all around her dresser. She had no clue how her last pill would get out of the bottle onto the dresser or the floor, but she knew she hadn't taken it. When she took her pill that morning, she eyed the last pill in the bottle, and hit up a guy she knew by the name of Jason.

Being that she'd been on the pills for nine months, Lyric decided to ease up on going to the doctor for a few months. She told herself that it would look good on her behalf to tell her doctor that she'd tolerated the pain for months without using strong drugs. By the time she went back to the doctor, she'd be good for another few months. Being that it was so easy to get prescription drugs off the street, Lyric decided to go that route for a minute. When she hit Jason up, he informed her that it would be another day before he got any pills in. So Lyric decided to go as long as she could without taking her last pill. When her hands became clammy and she broke out into a cold sweat, she knew it was time for her last pill, but it wasn't in the bottle.

Jules walked into the room with his left hand bandaged. "What's good?"

Lyric looked down at his hand. "What happened?"

Jules looked down at his hand. "Playing basketball with Jacques. I think I sprained my wrist. I'm trying to hold off on going to the doctor, so I just wrapped it up and took one of your pills."

Lyric had to literally bite her tongue to keep from going off. "Jules, why would you take my last pill without asking me if I would need it. I take those pills for a reason." Her tone remained even, but he could clearly see that she was agitated.

"My bad. I didn't think you took 'em like that anymore. You don't really do hair like that anymore, and I never hear you complain about the pain."

"I don't complain about the pain because I take the pills." She gritted. Lyric walked over to their bed and sat down on the edge of it. She needed to think. Who could she get some pills from? Lyric ran her clammy hands up and down her pants' leg.

Jules watched her with his eyebrow raised. It had been months since her hands cramped up. He knew when her hands were hurting because it was hard for her to do anything, even get the top off the pill bottle. When she was having an episode, he had to do things for her. Lyric would damn near be in tears. He hadn't seen her in pain in a long time. To his knowledge, a person took pain medication to deal with pain, not prevent it. If she was taking the pills on a regular basis, before she even started hurting, how did she know she still needed the medication? Lyric was a trooper though, so he didn't want to jump to conclusions. Maybe she really did need the pills.

"I should have asked. Are your hands hurting you now?"

"Yes." Lyric didn't even look him in the eyes. She just rocked slightly back and forth. Jules didn't want his wife to be uncomfortable, but he made a mental note to watch her and those pills. "Aight. I'll see if Jacques can get you a pill or two until you can get to the doctor."

A look of relief instantly washed over Lyrics' face. "Thank you, baby."

Jules left the room to call his brother. Jules knew firsthand the dangers of addiction. He served addicts for years, and he even started depending on coke after his father died. Coke almost destroyed him. He hoped that he was overreacting, but he was going to keep a close eye on Lyric.

Chapter Five

J2's eyes narrowed as he pulled from the blunt that sat between his lips. After taking a hefty toke, he held the smoke in his lungs for a good five seconds as he eyed the beaten and bloody man in front of him. After blowing the weed smoke from his lungs, J2 scratched his eyebrow. "Where the fuck is my shit, Marcellus? And let this be the last time that I ask you," J2's voice held a no-nonsense tone. Patience was something that he didn't have a lot of, and he'd been questioning Marcellus for ten minutes with no luck.

Marcellus hustled for him, and he'd fucked up work twice in the last two months. The first time he didn't have J2's money, he claimed that he got arrested, but when J2 checked, there was no record of his arrest.

Wanting to be certain before he killed the nigga, he gave him one more pack. The shit was way less than his usual amount, and he still didn't even bring back the money from that. He came at J.J. with a sob story that he got robbed. J2 was tired of playing with him. He knew losses were a part of the game, but he was using this one as a teaching experience. J2 didn't like getting his hands dirty, but he did what was needed when necessary. He let J.J. and Kareem beat Marcellus for a good five minutes while his ten employees watched. Once they were done beating him, J2 asked him question after question, even though the man was damn near unconscious.

"M-m-my mother t-t-took it. She's a fiend. I swear I'll get all your money back," Marcellus panted in a voice barely above a whisper.

"Nah, see that's where you got me fucked up." J2 hit the blunt again. "I rarely give second chances, and you made me see why I don't. You played me two fuckin' times. Like I'm just some sucka out this bitch. Then you have the nerve to ask me to give you a third chance to fuck me over. That lil' paper I lost off you is going to have to be charged to the game. I'm not an unreasonable guy though. I'll give you a few seconds to get right with God."

"Lil' Jules please man. I swear—" He was silenced by a bullet to the head.

J2 kissed his teeth. "I told this nigga to get right with God, and he begging me. Hardheaded. That's why he dead now." J2 eyed his workers. "Anybody else that gets the bright idea to cross me for my work, you'll meet the same fate. Kareem, Lawrence, clean this shit up," he commanded before walking outside.

Being that J2 was so quiet and laid back, when people saw him get buck for the first time, it often surprised them. People were skeptical when they found out the lanky young man with barely any facial hair was the one running the show. He looked young, no matter how mature he acted. Plus, even when he used slang, or smiled and show-cased his grills, anyone with good hearing could tell that J2 was smart as fuck. He didn't need paper, pencil, or calculators to solve some of the most complex math problems. The man was borderline genius. When acts of violence sometimes bothered even the most hardened criminal, J2 didn't blink when he had to put in work. It came with the game, and the game was what he'd always wanted to be a part of. He was his father's past reincarnated.

J.J. walked out behind him. "How you want to handle this shit going forward?"

"The shit may be tedious, but I'm no longer waiting for niggas to be done with the work before they pay me. When they make the first half, I want it. After that, once the pack is gone, they come with the other half." J2's workers had two ways that they got off dope.

Some posted up at one of his trap houses and the fiends came to get their fix that way. It didn't take long for word to spread as far as traps were concerned, and the area would eventually get hot, meaning police started lurking and watching. J2 made it a point to switch trap houses every five or six months. He also had hustlers that were mobile. It didn't matter if a fiend called them and was thirty miles away; if he or she was spending enough, they'd pull up to go serve them. Some people straight copped the work from J2 and paid him for it, and that was that. They had their own clientele and moved the dope how they wanted to move it. Then there were people that worked for J2 and sold his dope for him. They got a cut from each ounce that they sold. Marcellus was one of those workers, and he kept fucking up J2's money, so he had to go.

J.J. nodded his head slowly. "That's a good idea. Those niggas were scared shitless in there. I don't think you'll have any more problems."

"Let's hope not, but I'm out. I have homework to do."

J.J. chuckled. "You the only muhfucka I know that will body a nigga then run off to do homework. Be easy. I'm going to make sure these fools handling shit right, and then I'm leaving too." J.J. was older than J2 by a little less than a year, but he had no problem letting his cousin take the lead.

Hustling was in his blood too, but prior to J2 hitting him up with the idea, J.J. was content being a spoiled rich kid. He wanted no parts of college, and he was living off the money that Jacques had set aside for him. All of Jacques' kids were rich by their tenth birthdays. J.J. kept telling himself that he was going to take some of the money and start a business, but he didn't really know what he wanted to do. He loved shopping and was thinking of opening up a men's clothing store, when his cousin came to him with the proposition to be his right-hand man. Wasn't no pussy in Jacques Jr., so he readily agreed.

Walking over to his gold BMW, he pulled his ringing phone from his pocket and saw that Arbrianna was calling him. "What's good?" he asked. Arbrianna was a lil' freak that he'd been fucking for ten months. She had a big sexual appetite and a banging ass body.

"I need some weed. And some dick." She spoke seductively into the phone, causing J.J.'s dick to jump. Arbrianna's sex game was off the charts. Shorty could suck a mean dick, her pussy stayed gushy, and she wasn't afraid to try new shit.

"Aight. I'll be through there in about fifteen minutes. Be naked." J.J. met Arbrianna hanging around the college campus with J2. She was in her third year. She was a true freak. She smoked hella weed and popped pills sometimes, but she was determined to get a degree in Political Science. J.J. didn't know what she was going to do with it, but all that mattered was that she wanted it.

J.J. was much like his father in a lot of ways. He was a ladies' man. J.J. loved women, and the women loved him. After stopping to get a box of condoms and some cigars, J.J. pulled up at Arbrianna's spot. She lived with her cousin in a two-bedroom townhouse. J.J.'s finger was still pressed on the doorbell when the door slowly swung open. "Damn," he mumbled as his eyes traveled up and down Arbrianna's copper colored frame. This was why he fucked with her.

She answered the door dressed in nothing but gray Calvin Klein panties. After giving him a sexy smirk, Arbrianna turned on her heels and headed for her bedroom. J.J. followed and closed the door behind him. After kicking off his shoes, he pulled weed from his pocket and passed the baggie and cigars to Arbrianna. He loved watching her roll the blunt. Especially when she wrapped her lips around the cigar paper to seal it. The shit turned him on every time.

"How was your day?" she asked him as she broke the weed up.

"It was straight. What about you?" J.J. ran his hand along her thick thigh.

"Today was a good day. I got an A on a test and a high B on a paper that I had to turn in."

"Word. You gotta handle that high B though. If yo' ass want that Fendi purse, you gotta make the Dean's list, baby."

"I am. I have three more weeks to pull my grades up. I'm getting that purse. Watch."

Once the blunt was rolled, Arbrianna and J.J. sat and talked as they smoked. She was chill and laid back, and they vibed well together. As soon as the blunt was gone, she looked at him with low eyes as she bit on her bottom lip. He knew what that look meant.

"Get that shit," he said in a low voice. She wanted dick, and she could damn sure have it.

He would never have to tell her twice. Arbrianna took her manicured hands and pulled J.J.'s dick from the confinement of his jeans. Leaning over, she licked her lips before taking him into her mouth. As she bobbed her head up and down slowly, she hummed on his dick, causing him to hiss. Arbrianna cupped his balls with her hands as she sped up the pace. After a few moments, she stopped sucking and spit on the dick before taking him back into her mouth. The head was slow and sloppy just like he liked it. J.J. grabbed a handful of her hair and thrust his hips as he began to fuck her face. Arbrianna loved that shit, and she didn't gag or choke once. Challenging herself to take all of him, she refused to let the dick win.

When he couldn't take anymore, J.J. gently yanked her head all the way back. He stood up and pulled a condom from his pocket. Arbrianna could tell he was sober. To her, weed didn't count. Anytime J.J. was drunk, he slid up in her raw, and she loved that shit. But on this day, his body was free from alcohol, and he made sure to wear protection. Once he'd rolled the Magnum onto his shaft, J.J. pulled her to the edge of the bed. He remained in a standing position as he placed her legs over his shoulders and dug into her gushy tunnel.

"Fucckkkkkkkkkkkkk," Arbrianna moaned as she cupped her breasts in her hands. She loved fucking J.J. It was something that they did at least four times a week, and that still wasn't enough for her. If it were up to her, she'd fuck him every day.

"Open that pussy up for daddy." He gritted as he thumbed her clit with his hand.

"Jacquessssss." He loved the way she said his name using a melodic tune. That only made him drill into her harder and faster.

"Damn this pussy good," he chanted as he fucked her in an aggressive manner. Pulling himself out of her, Jacques lay on the bed and pulled her on top of him.

Arbrianna loved being on top. She rode him fast and hard as her breasts bounced up and down, and he gripped her ass cheeks so hard that his nails were digging into her soft flesh, but she didn't care. After throwing her head back, she let out a throaty moan. "I'm about to cum, baby," she whined.

"Me too. Let that shit go." J.J. gritted as he smacked her ass.

Arbrianna moved her hips in a circular motion as she leaned down and placed her lips onto his. After easing her tongue into his mouth, the pair engaged in a sloppy tongue kiss that had fireworks emitting from her core. The way her pussy muscles gripped his dick like a vice had him unable to hold back his seed.

"Fuccck," he groaned as a powerful orgasm rocked his core and sent his seed shooting into the condom.

Out of breath, Arbrianna smirked as she rolled off of him. As if on cue, his phone rang. Even though he looked at it, J.J. had no plans of answering until he saw that it was Stacy. "Yo," he said out of breath after he accepted the call.

"Hey. What are you doing? You sound out of breath?"

"Shit. Smoking and bullshitting. What's good?"

"Can you come over tonight? I'm cooking a special meal for you."

"Why didn't you let me know earlier?" he questioned. J.J. knew if he went to Stacy's crib, she would want to end the night with sex. Being that they didn't have sex, he didn't want to deny her, but Arbrianna had just drained him. J.J. wasn't even certain that he'd be able to get it up again. But he didn't want to disappoint Stacy. She was the good girl type. She was smart, selective about who she gave her time to, and she'd been celibate for two years before meeting J.J. She wasn't a girl that you wanted to mess up with because J.J. knew when he was ready to settle down, it would make sense to settle down with someone like her.

"I was so busy running around trying to get everything prepared that it slipped my mind. Are you busy?" She sounded disappointed.

"I won't be in a minute. I'll be through there. Give me about two hours."

Just like that, Stacy's voice turned perky. "Okay. See you soon."

J.J. ended the call, and Arbrianna sucked her teeth. "Let me guess, that was my sister."

J.J. stood up and peeled the condom from his dick. "Yeah it was. What's the problem?"

Arbrianna turned her head and glared at the wall. "There isn't one."

Never mind that he'd fucked her first. In the back of her mind, Arbrianna knew that if J.J. had to choose, he'd choose Stacy. No matter how good she fucked and sucked him, he always catered to bitch ass Stacy. With a newfound attitude, Arbrianna stood up and headed for the bathroom. Fuck J.J. and her sister.

Chapter Six

"You had fun today?" Tre asked Reign as they left the studio. After mulling over the decision for a few days, she finally decided to go to Miami with him. Jayla was with her, and she had money. If anything went wrong, she'd be on the first plane smoking back to North Carolina. Why not enjoy a free trip to Miami with a famous rapper? After all, this was the time of her young life when she was supposed to be living her best life.

"I did." Being in the studio for five hours watching rappers put songs together might seem boring to some, but Reign found it exciting. Not to mention, she lowkey felt like a celebrity herself. Her last ten snaps had more than 1,000 views. Her Instagram followers were up to 8,000. Reign had to make her account private from jealous ass trolls. Some people were big mad that Tre was showing interest in her and they would put rude comments under her pictures, calling her ugly, or anything that they felt may hurt her feelings.

"Cool. We gotta go back to the room and get changed. I gotta do a walk through at Liv tonight. Tomorrow I have a radio interview, and after that we can go shopping and shit."

"Sounds good."

Jayla had her own hotel room, so Reign chose to get dressed in her room to keep her company. One of Tre's homies, Choppa, was trying to get at Jayla. He was just a hype man, a part of the crew or whatever, so his money definitely wasn't as long as Tre's, but he was cute. He stood six feet one with honey colored skin and pretty, curly hair. His entire upper body was covered in tattoos; he even had two on his face. He was cute enough for Jayla to flirt with. That way, she didn't feel like a third wheel. Jayla was a nice size ten with thick thighs and wide hips. She felt if her stomach were flat she'd be perfect, but her father told her daily that she was already perfect. She just hated having to wear Spanx whenever she wanted to wear tight dresses. Jayla also hated her A cup breasts, but Jacques paid her half of the bills at the apartment, and he put $1,000 a month in her account. He also paid her credit card bills. She didn't have enough cash to pay for her own surgery, and if she used a credit card, he'd have a fit. Jayla wanted to be a teacher, and it was her personal goal to graduate from college, get a job, and get surgery.

"Bitch, you know we got bitches big mad," Jayla said to Reign as she shimmied into her form fitting nude dress. Taking after her father, Jayla had light-skin and a broad nose. Two small moles decorated her face. One on her bottom lip and her the other on her left cheek. Her stomach wasn't as flat as she wanted it to be, but Jacques refused to give her money for surgery. He told her she was beautiful the way she was.

Reign ran a brush through her long tresses. "I don't give a fuck. I had to turn my comments off earlier because I got tired of blocking people. Some idiot called me a groupie and said I fuck for trips to Miami. Muhfuckas got me fucked up." Most things rolled off Reign's back.

She didn't give a damn who didn't like her, but her local haters knew she wasn't a hoe, and she didn't have to chase niggas for money. The strangers from the internet however, were ready to toss her in the category with gold diggers. They saw her with Tre and assumed she was looking for a come up. It was irritating, but she knew it came with the territory.

"You liking Choppa?" She decided to change the subject.

"He's cool. I guess it won't really matter if I like him or not though. Like, you think these niggas really gon' stick around, or are we just their pastime for the moment?"

"I definitely don't think either of them are looking for girlfriends, and I'm not interested in being a part of a harem. I say we just have fun for the moment and not expect too much."

"Agreed." Jayla slipped her feet into some nude heels. "Now, let's take some shots. Tonight needs to be super litty."

Back in his room, Tre had Choppa keeping watch while he got head from a girl in the bathroom of his hotel suite. He already knew what type of girl Reign was, so he wasn't expecting to have sex with her during her visit. He still had needs though and plenty of women that wanted to fulfill them. An Instagram model had been hitting him up ever since she saw that he was in town. He set it up for her to come to his room once he found out that Reign was spending time in Jayla's room in an effort to keep her from being lonely. If he busted a nut, he'd be able to sleep that night without becoming frustrated with Reign for not giving it up. He was becoming used to the women that wouldn't deny him no matter what he asked, so while he could appreciate Reign, he knew that once he got horny, that appreciation would fly out of the window.

"Fuckkkkk, girl." Tre licked his lips as Anonda deep throated his thick dick. "Do that shit," he moaned as he pressed his back against the bathroom door. Shorty was gagging and humming on his dick making the experience pleasurable as hell for him.

She had no idea that as soon as he came, she'd be dismissed and not thought of again. Anonda had a few major players on her team that kept her pockets laced. She fucked with a dope boy, a football player, and a business owner. She thought a rapper was about to be added to her list, but she was sadly mistaken. Using her hand, she slid it up and down his saliva coated shaft and jacked him off as she sucked.

Tre's toes curled, and his stomach tightened as he was brought closer to reaching his peak. "Fuck, bitch!" He placed his hand on the back of her head and pushed her face into his crotch. His body rocked slightly as an orgasm set off fireworks in his body and sent his seed shooting down her throat. "Ummmmmmmm," he groaned as she sucked out every drop.

Anonda swallowed every drop that he left on her tongue and stood up with a smile gracing her honey colored face. She was gorgeous indeed, and Dr. Miami had done her body right. She wasn't what Tre wanted on his arm though. He vowed to never wife a female that had been passed around any industry, be it the music industry or among athletes. "That shit was fye. 'Preciate you, but I gotta get ready to go."

Anonda didn't let her disappointment show. "That's cool. What are you doing after the show? I need the proper amount of time to really make you feel good," she cooed seductively.

"Nah, I'm good. What you already showed me was amazing. I'm fine with that. My man will show you out. I need to jump in the shower."

No longer able to hide her disdain, Anonda scoffed. "Wow." She wasn't dismissed or disrespected often, but when she was, she didn't like it. There was really nothing she could do about it though. That's what happened when you threw yourself at various men. Not all of them responded the same. She opened up the door for contempt from others. "That's what it is then," she snapped and left the bathroom.

Tre chuckled as he turned the shower water on and began to undress. She had handled rejection well. In the past, he had women to straight go the hell off. He had two children to take care of. Even though he and his baby mamas hadn't been together in years, he made sure they were straight simply because they had his kids. His first baby mama, Taylor, was married, so she didn't ask for much. He gave her $2,500 a month and provided medical insurance for their son, so she was more than happy with that. His second baby mama, Nesha, he bought her a car, paid her rent every month, and gave her $2,500 a month for their daughter. Every now and then, she hit him up for a bag or something, but she wasn't too worrisome, and that's how he wanted to keep it.

He also took care of his mother. With all of that going on, Tre didn't have the desire to trick with a bunch of women or get caught up with one that had motives. He needed a woman like Reign on his team. Being single wasn't better than having in house pussy and a woman by your side down to ride for you. He just had to make sure the woman he chose didn't *need* him in order to come up. Reign wasn't the type of female that he had to worry about trapping him with a baby or no goofy shit like that. Of course, he'd still have fun with other women, but as long as he kept his indiscretions hidden, he was confident that he'd soon have her wrapped around his finger. She was a bad chick that he could show off with confidence knowing that she hadn't been ran through by other famous niggas. Reign was a keeper. He just had to play his cards right and do what it took to keep her.

While the group was waiting to be seated at a popular Miami restaurant, Tre wrapped his arms around Reign's waist and placed his face in the crook of her neck. Aside from sleeping in his arms, that was the most touching they'd ever done. They kept it light around each other, but out of the blue, Tre was being affectionate, and it made Reign a little nervous. She wasn't sure why she was nervous. She wasn't a virgin, but she wasn't going to sleep with Tre just because he was Tre da Don. After spending time with him, she had to admit that she did like him. Reign just didn't want to get her hopes up. Everywhere they went, women flirted with him shamelessly, like she wasn't even there.

They threw themselves at him and acted like he was the last man walking the Earth. Reign had always been confident, but even she was intimidated by some of the women that pined after Tre. She wasn't interested in fighting for a spot in his life. Either he wanted her for real or he didn't. They'd just come from the mall where he bought her two pairs of shoes, a necklace, and a dress. Being that it was her last night in Miami, Reign wondered if he was suddenly being touchy feely because he wanted sex before she left.

"Damn, I wish you didn't have to go. I have four shows next week, then I'll have two weeks off. What if I come chill with you for a few days?"

Reign turned her head in an effort to see his face. "Really?"

He lifted his face from the space between her jaw and shoulder. "What you mean really? I want to spend time with you, but I know you got school and shit. Instead of asking you to come to me, I can come to you."

Reign wasn't the kind of female that asked the 'so what are we?' question, but she really wanted to know. Tre seemed to be putting forth a lot of effort, but men had done stranger things. It seemed dumb to pursue a woman hard as hell and then waste her time, but men did it all the time. Reign wasn't interested in having her time wasted.

"I get that, but I mean..." her voice trailed off while she tried to think of the right words to say. "I'm just saying that, you're famous. You travel a lot, we don't live in the same city, and everywhere you go, women are after you. It's not even feasible for us to have anything serious, yet you want to invest all this time. Why?"

Tre walked around and stood directly in front of Reign. "Why? Damn, shawty, you say it like us having something is the strangest thing in the world. It's not feasible? That's bullshit. Yes, I'm famous, and I travel a lot, but I also get down time. It might not be the easiest thing to do, but we can make it work. I can come to you as much as I can, and when you're not in school, you can come to me. And as far as the women, fuck them. I've had my share of hoes. I'm tired of that shit."

Reign studied his facial expression. He seemed sincere, but she wasn't sure. Maybe he just had a good ass talk game. She barely trusted college guys, so she damn sure didn't trust a famous rapper. Reign wasn't against love. In fact, she wanted a love like her mother had with her stepfather Jules. She didn't get to see the love shared between her biological father, Country, and her mother, but what she witnessed between Jules and her mother, she wanted. Jules didn't play about her mother, and everybody knew it. As far as Reign knew, he didn't cheat, and whatever her mother wanted, she got. Once Reign found a man to love her like Jules loved Lyric, she'd be all in, but she was also smart enough to know that men like her father were super rare.

"I hear you talking. When you get the down time, let me know. I'd be down for a visit from you."

After the group ate dinner, they headed back to the hotel and did their own thing. Reign and Tre chilled in the jacuzzi and had drinks. They then took a shower together and his busy schedule caught up with him because before they could even finish sharing a blunt, he was asleep with his mouth half open, snoring lightly. Reign sat on the bed beside him Indian style and stared at him as she pulled from the blunt. He was handsome as hell. This man was wanted by thousands of women, and she was there with him. He hadn't been arrogant or cocky. Not once had he disrespected her. He made sure she was straight always, and he spent money on her like it was nothing. And on top of all of that, he hadn't pressured her for sex. As she inhaled the powerful kush and enjoyed the high that it took her mind and body on, she smirked. After hitting the blunt once more, Reign stood up and pulled her camisole over her head, revealing her perky B cup breasts. After pulling down her thong and stepping out of it, she straddled Tre and stared down at him with hooded, lust-filled eyes.

Tre was tired as hell and the weed hadn't helped. He could feel someone on top of him but rather than opening his eyes, he instinctively brought his hands up and gripped her waist. Reign leaned forward so they were chest to chest, and she placed a soft kiss on Tre's lips. That made his lids flutter open, and the sight of a naked Reign on top of him instantly made his dick stiffen. He moved his hands up to the small of her back. Reign kissed him again, but that time she parted his lips with her tongue. They engaged in a sensual tongue kiss that had her grinding on him. Tre pushed his Polo pajama pants past his hips without breaking the kiss. As soon as his dick sprang out, Reign climbed off his lap.

"You got condoms?" she asked.

Tre knew that unprotected sex was intimate. Some niggas did it just because, but fucking females raw that a man didn't want to get open, was dangerous. And not just because of the threat of STDs. "I can pull up my chart from the health portal at my doctor's office. I'm clean baby. I was just tested two months ago. I haven't hit anybody raw since then, but I trust you, and I won't get you pregnant. I don't want to use a condom with you, bae."

Why was he so damn sexy? Reign wanted to scream. Even though she was on birth control, she felt like in terms of who he was, she was playing a dangerous game, but her young ass was all in. Climbing back onto his lap, she hovered above his crotch and positioned herself just right to slide down on his meaty tool. It wasn't that long, but it was fat, and it filled her up.

"Shit," Tre moaned as Reign's pussy muscles gripped his dick. Shorty was super wet and super tight.

With admiration, he watched her sexy ass do her thing as she rode him with the skill of an equestrian. He noticed the trail of butterflies going down her left side. "Fuck, you so fuckin' sexy. Shit," he moaned as she bit her bottom lip.

Wanting to be sure he gave her something to think about when they were apart, Tre flipped her onto her back and pushed one of her legs all the way back before diving into her middle. The headboard slammed into the wall as he fucked her hard and fast. "Treeee!" He finally made her whine, and it stroked his ego.

Dipping his head low, his tongue circled her hardened nipple, and she began to buck uncontrollably as she had an orgasm. "Ohhhhhh!" she cried as she arched her back, and honey poured from her middle.

"Fuck yes. Wet this dick up, baby. Shit, you feel so damn good," Tre grunted before crashing his lips into hers. They kissed for a good five minutes before he placed his lips against her ear. "You on birth control?"

Unable to speak, Reign nodded her head furiously.

"So I can nut all in this pussy?" He breathed as he felt an orgasm building.

He was fucking her so hard that Reign damn near bit her tongue. "Yesssss!" she squealed.

"Uhhhhhhhhh!" Tre growled as he sprayed Reign's womb full of his seed. "Damn, this pussy good," he stated and collapsed on top of her. There was no doubt in his mind that he had her.

Chapter Seven

Tre for sure accomplished what he set out to do, because Reign thought about him the entire plane ride back to North Carolina. Every time she thought about the sex they had, her vagina throbbed. Tre had fucked the shit out of her, and she was hoping and praying that he meant what he said, and they could do it again. Once her and Jayla got off the plane, they headed for Reign's Lexus, and she took Jayla home. She then headed to her parents' house for Sunday dinner. When she pulled up in the driveway, Reign noticed that J2 hadn't arrived yet. As soon as she entered the house, the aroma from the food smacked her in the face. Reign entered the living room and found Jules watching football and smoking a blunt.

"Hey, Dad," she greeted in a chipper tone as she sat down on the white leather couch.

From the look that Jules gave her, she could tell instantly that he wasn't pleased. "Why you didn't tell us you were going to Miami with that rapping nigga?" Jules asked in a very low tone, but anger danced in his eyes, making his true feelings obvious.

Reign lowkey wished her mother was in the room to come to her rescue, as she always did when her father was overreacting. "I didn't think it really mattered. Jayla was with me."

Jules eyes narrowed. "Jayla was with you? Fuck that mean? You didn't tell me you were going there for him because you knew I wouldn't approve. Right?"

Reign's eyes dropped to the carpeted floor. That's exactly why she didn't tell him. After staring at the floor for ten seconds, she held her head high and looked her father in the eyes. "Dad, I'm not a child anymore. I'm in my last year of college. I live on my own. I'm an adult. I didn't think I had to run every single thing by you." Reign made sure to use the most respectful tone she could. Jules didn't play that fuck shit. Even as grown as she was, she was still scared of his ass.

"Out of all the niggas to be with, why a rapper, Reign? You know that nigga is out here hitting every groupie in sight. I know you're not a groupie because I raised you better than that. Plus, that fuck ass nigga damn sure ain't worth more than me," Jules growled. Reign had to smile at him. There wasn't a man walking the planet like Jules Baptiste.

"Dad, you always told me not to date street niggas, and I never have. Can you trust that I can take care of myself? Please?" It was weird to her that she was older than J2, and he was running a whole drug empire, but Jules was mad because she was dating a rapper.

Before he could answer. The front door opened, and seconds later, J2 came into view. Dressed in a white Versace shirt and dark denim jeans, he was the spitting image of his father. Jules leaned forward to smash what was left of his blunt into the glass ashtray in front of him. "And this lil' nigga. You knew about this Tre da Don cat? Why you ain't whooped his ass?" Jules questioned his son and was dead ass serious.

"I started to get him at the club, Dad. I swear I did, but Reign texted me and told me everything was aight, and it wasn't that deep."

"What wasn't that deep?" Lyric asked, entering the room followed by Bella. Lyric was dressed in army fatigue joggers, a black fitted tee, and black sneakers. Her box braids were up in a bun, and she didn't look a day over thirty. Her eyebrows were contoured to the gawds, and her mink lashes looked natural and made her eyes pop. On the left side of her neck was a tattoo that said Jules. From her ears hung large gold hoops. Lyric looked like a pretty ass around the way girl, rather than the mother of two grown kids.

"Maaaa," Reign groaned. "Daddy is mad that I went to Miami with Tre, and he telling J2 to beat him up," she whined, hoping her mother would take her side.

Lyric's gaze swept back and forth from Jules to their son. "Really, Jules? And J2 if you touch that boy, I'm going to beat your ass. Leave this girl alone. She is not a child. I trust that she can handle herself." Lyric walked over to Reign and wrapped her arms around her daughter's shoulders, causing Reign to grin.

Jules' upper lip curled into a snarl and he stood up. "Whatever. If that nigga get outta line even one time, I'm stomping him the fuck out." He reached out his arms for Bella and she walked into his embrace. "You can't date until you're thirty. If you do that for me, I'll buy you a Rolls Royce."

Bella smiled big and wide. "Okay, Daddy."

Lyric chuckled. "Yeah, we'll see how long that lasts. Y'all come eat."

"Dad, I don't want to leave," Arianna stated with tears in her eyes as she looked up at her father. She was used to arguing between her parents, but she was stunned when Kymani told her they were moving out. Arianna loved her room, she loved the house they lived in, and she loved their neighborhood. Even though Kymani showed her a nice three-bedroom house, she didn't want to live there.

She wasn't trying to cause conflict between her parents. She loved them equally, but she just didn't want to leave the only house she'd ever lived in. Their house was huge, and out of six houses on the street, there were only two black families. The neighbor to the left of them was a retired NFL player, and his daughter Bria was Arianna's best friend.

"It's okay, babe. You can stay with me. You know as long as I'm here, you can be here too." Jacques did his best to comfort his daughter.

"I don't want Mom to be mad at me. Can't the two of you just make it work?" she begged, but deep down in her heart, she wasn't banking on it. There was always a possibility that they could work it out, but Arianna wasn't a kid anymore. She knew that sometimes marriages ended. That was just life. Bria's parents were together, but they didn't even sleep in the same room anymore.

"I don't want you stressing. Whatever is supposed to happen will, but no matter what happens, I love you, and I always got your back. Aight?"

Arianna nodded and headed upstairs towards her room. Jacques sat on the couch and waited for Kymani to pull up. She'd been getting her place situated for the past few days, and this was supposed to be the day that her and Arianna moved in. If she wanted to leave, she could go, but she wasn't making Arianna go anywhere. Even though Kymani came along and helped him a great deal, he was a single father when they met. Arianna would be just fine with him. Getting her to accept that would probably be a hard task though. Ever since Jacques went to Miami and talked to his aunt Vi, he'd been calmer. When she revealed to him that Kymani didn't give him anything that would hurt him, his desire to wring her neck went away. After he threw up and had irritating diarrhea for a few hours, he was back to normal.

Even though he hadn't cheated in years, Jacques knew he was to blame for Kymani feeling like she needed to go through such drastic measures to get him to tell her the truth. He still had mad love for her, but he wasn't so sure they were meant to be together forever. It wasn't about another woman. Jacques wasn't even sure what it was about. Maybe they just had to accept the fact that people sometimes fall out of love. It was nothing that Kymani had done, and maybe she did deserve someone better. Jacques finally decided to let her be free to find that man, but he was aware that would make him look like the bad guy also. He didn't want to break Kymani's heart, but she wanted the truth, so she'd gotten it.

Jacques saw her car pulling up in the driveway, and he knew the news that he was about to give her would make her angry. When she came in the house, she looked tired. "I'm just here to get Arianna. Here's your key." Kymani began removing the house key from the keychain in her hand.

When Jacques spoke, his voice was soft. "You don't have to give me the key back. Kymani, Arianna doesn't want to go, and I told her she doesn't have to. I mean, of course she can stay with you some nights, but she doesn't want to move out, and I'm not going to make her."

Kymani's eyes filled with tears. If she knew one thing, it was that Jacques didn't play about his kids. The worst thing she could do was try and force Arianna from the house when she was old enough to make her own decisions. It wasn't fair though. Jacques had done her wrong. He obviously wanted out of the marriage, so he should have to sit in that big house alone. Kymani shouldn't have to be alone. In a way, it felt as if everyone were betraying her. Even her own child. As soon as the tears spilled over her eyelids, she brushed them away angrily.

"It's just crazy to me that I'm the one being punished. Me. After everything I did. I—"

"Kymani, I don't want to hear that shit," Jules damn near growled, but his tone remained low. "Every time you get mad, you throw up in my face how you helped me to raise my kids that weren't yours, and I'm tired of hearing the shit. Yes, you helped me, and I love you for that, but gah damn. How many times did I try to set you free? How many times did I tell you that maybe you should leave? You could have left at any time if the shit was too much for you. I didn't hold a gun to your head and make you help me raise my kids. I was there every day. One thing I never will be is a deadbeat. You had me, you had my mom, J.J.'s grandparents and nannies. Don't act like you were kept hostage up in a crib raising my kids while I sat back and did nothing, 'cause then I get pissed off."

"That's not what I meant, and you know it. But damn, I rode hard as hell for you, and this is the thanks that I get?"

Jacques shot up from the couch like a rocket. "The fuck do you want from me? Huh? You want me to stay in a marriage that I don't want to be in to show you appreciation? Fuck outta here! Kymani, you wanted the truth, and this is as raw as it gets. I don't want to be married anymore, and my daughter doesn't want to leave this house. You are free to come over anytime you want, and I will tell her that she has to stay with you at least three nights a week. I'll even help you pay your bills at the crib, but this shit with us is done."

Kymani let out an angry chuckle as tears filled her eyes. "Fuck you, Jacques Baptiste. I wish I'd never met your ass." She turned around and stormed away from the house, leaving Jacques to wonder why he just couldn't get shit right.

Stacy sat with her back against the headboard of her bed with tears swimming in her eyes. This was the second time in a week that J.J.'s dick wouldn't get hard for her. It was making her feel very insecure. Was he not attracted to her anymore? With her mocha colored skin and high cheekbones, she was always being complimented on her looks. Her body wasn't perfect, her thick thighs held some cellulite and her stomach held stretch marks from weight gain a few years ago. She started working out and was now a size eight, but she still had the memories of her muffin top. None of those things had ever been an issue when it came to her and J.J. having sex. He was the second man that she'd ever had sex with, but he was the best she'd ever had. Stacy always prided herself on being one of the good girls that didn't give it up without a commitment, but after J.J. talked her out of her panties once, she was hooked, and commitment or not, he could get it whenever he wanted.

He was in the bathroom, and she was crying. Being horny and frustrated didn't go well with feeling rejected. His phone started lighting up, and Stacy could see that someone was calling him, but his phone wasn't ringing or vibrating. Stacy let out an angry chuckle. He had the phone on silent. Stacy wasn't dumb. She knew that J.J. was a ladies' man, and she tried not to let it bother her. It did though. It bothered her a lot. Still, he was discreet with his dirt, so a part of her hoped that he wasn't out in the streets doing much. Stacy knew that was wishful thinking though. Looking over at the phone, her eyebrows dipped low as hell to see that her sister was calling him. Her and Arbrianna weren't the closest, but they were sisters nonetheless. Arbrianna knew about her and J.J. so why in the hell was she calling him? Just as the phone stopped ringing and a text came through, J.J. emerged from the bathroom with a sheepish look on his face. He knew that Stacy was upset, but he couldn't help it. Arbrianna's sexual appetite had been crazy lately. Normally, he could satisfy multiple women with ease, but for some reason, the past few days had been too much for him, and the shit was lowkey embarrassing.

"Why is my sister calling your fucking phone?" Stacy asked as her bottom lip quivered. J.J. knew she was pissed because Stacy rarely cursed.

Fuck! He hardly ever left a room without his phone, and shit like this was the reason why. "I don't know," he lied lamely, praying that she would let it go. Stacy wasn't the argumentative type, so he really hoped she'd drop it. Because of her calm nature, he'd never had to turn up on her. He wouldn't even feel right barking on a person as docile as Stacy, but he would.

"Well, call her back and put her on speaker phone. We can find out together," she replied adamantly, crossing her arms underneath her breasts.

J.J. tried to take control of the situation. "Chill, shawty. Since when we been doing that? I'm single. You haven't been asking me questions. Why start now?"

"Up until now you've been able to juggle the shit you've been into, but your soft dick is telling me that either you don't like me anymore, or you're doing too much. Just in case that too much you're doing is with my sister, I need to know." Stacy snaked her neck and all. That was totally out of character for her preppy ass. J.J. knew that he'd messed up big time. Being dick deprived had turned Stacy into a completely different person.

Still trying to save face, J.J. kissed his teeth. "You really trying to play me right now. I told you a nigga is tired, but whatever. You're in the mood to argue, so I'm going home." J.J. picked his jeans up off the floor, but if he thought Stacy was backing down, he was wrong.

Reaching over on the nightstand, she grabbed her cell phone and angrily punched in her access code. Stacy eyed J.J. as she called her sister and put the call on speaker. "Why are you calling J.J.?" Stacy barked out as soon as Arbrianna answered. She knew how her sister got down, and if J.J. was fucking her, she'd never forgive them.

Arbrianna found Stacy's sudden gangsta attitude amusing. "Girl, if you don't get off my phone with that bullshit. I don't have to explain myself to you."

"Why are you calling the nigga I'm fucking?" Stacy yelled into the phone ignoring her sister's words.

On the other end of the phone, Arbrianna smiled. She'd never heard her sister say the word nigga. Stacy was big mad, and this was the shit she'd been waiting for. J.J. would be furious if she spilled the beans to Stacy on some messy shit, but clearly, she was being provoked. Now, she could hurt her feelings without J.J. being mad that she started shit. "'Cause I'm fucking him too, and I'm pregnant by him. Congratulations, auntie." Arbrianna dropped a bombshell that made both Stacy and J.J. stop dead in their tracks. Stacy even stopped breathing for a second. She held her breath and shot the man standing across from her daggers with her eyes. Her gut told her to leave J.J. where he stood the day that he approached her. She'd never been into hood niggas, and her common sense told her that dating one would be a huge mistake. However, she went against her better judgement, and look at her now.

J.J. wanted to reach through the phone and choke the shit out of Arbrianna. Stacy's eyes immediately darkened. She was in rare form. J.J. had never even seen her angry, let alone furious. Without another word to her sister, Stacy ended the call. Staring down at the black and white comforter on her bed, she tried to steady her breathing. "Get out," she demanded in a low tone.

Seconds before, J.J. had been ready to leave, but he didn't feel right leaving her like this. With the way he and Arbrianna had sex, her being pregnant was a huge possibility. Jacques had always told his son not to be like him. Here he was caught up between two women and had a baby on the way. Way not to be like his father. Arbrianna and Stacy were like night and day. He liked both of them for different reasons. When he approached Stacy, he knew she was Arbrianna's sister. He didn't give a damn though. J.J. played with fire, and as a result, his ass had gotten burned in a major way.

"Stacy liste—"

"Get out!" Stacy yelled from her gut. She yelled so loud and hard that her body shook, and the veins in her neck strained against her skin. She didn't want to cry. Crying in front of him would make her feel weak and lame, but Stacy knew she wouldn't be able to hold the tears back too much longer. She needed him away from her. Immediately.

J.J. finished getting dressed. He had a feeling that he'd never be able to make things right with her. He'd messed up in a major way. His next stop would be Arbrianna's to see what in the hell she was talking about. Right before he scooped his keys up off the dresser, Stacy jumped up off the bed. "Before you go, how long have you been fucking her? Huh? Tell me," she stated through gritted teeth as she pushed him in the chest.

J.J. let out a defeated sigh. "A minute. I was fucking her first. I got at you after her."

"Wow." Stacy let out an angry chortle. "Wow. So, I got her sloppy seconds. Wow. And she knew about me and you?"

"Not at first. When she found out, she was mad, but she didn't leave me alone."

"Of course she didn't. Get out. I fucking hate you," Stacy broke the promise to herself not to cry, and her shoulders shook up and down as she grieved.

"Stacy, I'm sorry," J.J. stated in a pitiful tone. He really did feel like shit watching her cry.

Stacy brushed past him, went into her bathroom, and slammed the door shut behind her. Every chance she got, Arbrianna made her life hell, but this was by far the worst betrayal ever.

"Why the fuck did you do that?" J.J. barked as he ran up on Arbrianna after she opened the door for him. The smirk that she wore on her face, pissed him off.

"Nigga, she called me with the bullshit."

"Why the fuck didn't you ignore her?" he screamed in her face. "You didn't have to tell her like that. That shit was childish!"

The smirk left Arbrianna's face and was immediately replaced with rage. "Nigga, fuck you. You the childish one! You fucked my sister! You knew she was my sister. Don't come at me like you some type of saint. You's a fucking fuck boy. I tell you what, go back to the bitch. Go be with her, and leave me the fuck alone. I don't need you!" she yelled at him with tears in her eyes. "Go make sure baby Stacy is okay, 'cause I'm good without you, nigga."

J.J. almost wanted to wrap his hands around Arbrianna's neck, but some crazy shit happened. His dick got hard. Stacy had tried for damn near fifteen minutes to get him hard. With no effort whatsoever, Arbrianna had managed to make him hard as steel. "Shut the fuck up." He gritted as he picked her up and took her to the bedroom.

Arbrianna wasn't surprised. Her and J.J.'s relationship was built on dysfunction. She tried to tell herself that she didn't care about anything that he did. All she wanted from him was dick and money, but no matter how much she lied to herself, J.J. had an effect on her. She loved him, but fear of him not loving her back caused her to hide her feelings. Arbrianna's pussy throbbed as J.J. tossed her on the bed and ripped her panties off.

"When you find out you were pregnant?" he asked as he undid his jeans. He was breathing hard from the task of carrying her coupled with his lust for her. The sexual chemistry hung thick in the air.

"A few hours ago," she mumbled as her chest heaved up and down.

As soon as dick was free, J.J. plunged into her without even taking his jeans all the way off. That's how urgent his need for her was. "You 'bout to have my baby?" He breathed before covering her lips with his and snaking his tongue into her mouth.

Arbrianna made an effort to nod her head as she widened her legs and welcomed J.J. to go deeper. No matter how volatile their relationship was, it was theirs, and she needed J.J. like she needed air to breathe.

Chapter Eight

It felt as if Jazlyn's bladder was about to burst, and that was the only thing that got her out of bed. As she dragged herself to the bathroom, she prayed for the darkness to pass. Jazlyn had stopped praying long ago, but today, she was desperate. She'd been battling a terrible bout of depression for the past two days, and she was mentally drained. Anything could trigger her to shut down, and this time the passing of her birthday did it. Her mother didn't call her, in fact no one did. Jazlyn was used to it. Mentally, she thought she'd prepared herself for it, but when she got on Instagram and saw J2 hugged up with Natori, her emotions got the best of her. It reminded Jazlyn that nobody gave a damn about her. It was something that she could normally push to the back of her mind, but it had become too overwhelming for her.

When Jazlyn stood up, she raised her arm and scrunched up her face in disapproval after she smelled her armpit. Depressed or not, she needed a shower. Jazlyn stripped the sheets from her bed, put them in the laundry basket, and went to take care of her personal hygiene. She had to admit that after brushing her teeth, taking a long hot shower, and rubbing her body down with lotion, she felt better. Once she dressed in a black, oversized night shirt that stopped just above her knees, she removed the rubber band from her thick hair and brushed it back up into a neat bun. "Better." She sighed, trying to force a smile. After lighting a candle, she made her bed up with fresh sheets, and tried to decide if she would warm up noodles or a can of Beefaroni. Even if she did feel a little better, Jazlyn wasn't in the mood to leave her dorm room, so options were few.

A knock at her door caused her to raise her eyebrow. Her roommate practically lived with her boyfriend, and Jazlyn rarely had company. As she headed to the door, she chalked it up as someone wanting to borrow something, and she had nothing to give. After she opened the door and saw J2 standing there looking good as ever, her breath hitched in her throat. He was the last person that she expected to see. Maybe he was there for his laptop.

"Hi," she managed to get out as he waltzed past her without waiting to be invited in. J2 was dressed in black jeans and a black hoodie. On his feet were wheat colored Timberlands, and his dreads were up in a bun. He looked and smelled heavenly.

"I just came to see what's up with you. Why haven't you been in class? You good?" He sat on the edge of her bed and peered at her.

"Um, yeah. I just haven't really felt like going. I'll be there tomorrow though."

"Why haven't you felt like coming?" he inquired. Initially, he always thought that not pressing the issue and giving her space would be best, but now he wasn't so sure. Maybe she needed someone to pry. It didn't take a genius to be able to look in Jazlyn's eyes and tell that she wasn't happy.

"I just haven't. I've been going through some things. Nothing major." She made the attempt at being evasive. From the way her eyes bounced around the room refusing to make contact, he knew that she was lying.

"Until you tell me what's good, I'm not leaving. I thought we were better than that, Jazlyn. Tell me what's wrong. I'm not really asking either."

Jazlyn wanted to be irritated, but she couldn't be. After all, that's what she wanted right? Someone to care. There he sat on her bed, showing genuine concern, and maybe all she needed was a release. Something told her that if she was too honest with him, she'd lose him as a friend. Maybe she could tell him just enough to get him off of her back. Jazlyn took a deep breath and walked over to sit beside him on the bed.

"I've just been in my feelings because yesterday was my birthday, and nobody cares. My mother didn't even call to wish me a happy birthday. It's not like I expected her to. I guess I'm just overreacting."

"Chill with that," J2 responded in a soft voice. "That's not overreacting. I think it's fucked up that your mom wouldn't even call. I'm grown as fuck, and my mom still makes a big deal of my birthday. What type of issues she got?"

Jazlyn stared at the floor and shook her head. "She's just not big on showing emotions. Never has been. She's never told me she loved me." Jazlyn knew she probably sounded pathetic, but everything she was saying was true. Why not get it off her chest? Maybe then, it would stop weighing her down.

"The marks on your legs, did she do that?" J2 asked, his voice full of concern.

This was where she didn't want to go. "I'm hungry. I was on my way out before you came," she lied. Jazlyn stood up, causing J2 to stand as well.

"Jazlyn," he stated in a warning tone.

Anger came out of nowhere and tears filled her eyes. "Yes, Jules. Yes. When I was twelve, she started pimping me out to different men. They would pay her to have sex with me, and when I would fight or resist, she would burn me with cigarettes. Are you happy?" Jazlyn had never revealed her past to anyone. She felt ashamed and dirty, but there was no taking the words back.

J2's eyes narrowed, and his chest heaved up and down. He was pissed. As pissed as he was the day the guy called her a bitch. It was then that Jazlyn knew without a shadow of a doubt that if she was ever in a bind, J2 would have her back with no questions asked, and that was all that she wanted in life. Someone that cared. Even if he belonged to someone else, having him as a friend was better than nothing at all. "She did what?" He seethed.

"That was many years ago. It only lasted for a few months. I got an STD, and the doctors were asking questions because I was so young. She stopped after that."

"Yoooo," J2 stated as he began to pace the floor. He didn't give a damn how long ago it was, if given the chance, he'd make Jazlyn's mom eat bullets. She was a poor excuse for a human being. He didn't know how to let shit like that slide. In his world, that type of shit warranted extreme consequences. No wonder Jazlyn looked like she didn't have a friend in the world most of the time.

Reaching out to touch his arm, even in her vulnerable state, Jazlyn attempted to calm him. "J2, I'm over it. Really."

He stopped pacing and looked at her. "That's the biggest lie I've ever heard. You're no way near over that shit, and if you let me, I'd make sure your mother died a slow and painful death, but you not even that type of person. So I'm going to push that disturbing shit to the back of my mind. Get dressed. We're about to celebrate your birthday."

Jazlyn raised her eyebrows. "What? Ju—"

His phone rang, and he cut her off before looking down at the phone screen. "Jazlyn, please quit making this shit difficult. Your stomach been growling since I got here. Can you just do what I asked?"

She decided to comply. J2 put his phone on silent and ignored a call from Natori. He'd have to hear her mouth later, but he felt what he was doing was more important than cupcaking on the phone. Jazlyn quickly got dressed in denim jeans, a denim blouse, and tan riding boots. Once she was dressed, J2 opened the door for her, and she exited her dorm room.

The entire fifteen-minute drive to the restaurant, the only noise in the car was Migos playing through the speakers. J2 pulled up at a Japanese restaurant Kanki, and they got out of the car. Jazlyn was feeling awkward as hell. She couldn't believe that she'd confessed to a man that she had a crush on, that she was raped at twelve-years-old and contracted an STD. That had to be one of the dumbest things that she'd ever done, but she couldn't take it back.

"What's something that you want for your birthday?" J2 asked once they had been seated and placed their drink orders.

"Um, nothing really. I just wanted it to be acknowledged. That's it," she responded nervously.

J2 chuckled. "I swear getting anything out of you is like pulling teeth. I'm not a stranger to you. We've been cool for months. You know me. Stop playing with me, man. When I ask you something, just stop all the extra shit, and tell me what I want to know." J2's tone held authority, but he didn't raise his voice at her.

"I don't *want* anything, Jules. About the only thing that I need is a laptop, and I've been using yours."

J2 nodded. "Okay, cool."

The first part of dinner was awkward, but Jazlyn eventually loosened up. Dinner was delicious, and J2 was sitting across from her looking more scrumptious than the food. Jazlyn felt like the luckiest girl in the world. Suddenly, her mother not calling on her birthday seemed irrelevant. When dinner was over, Jazlyn assumed J2 was taking her back to the dorm, so she was confused when he pulled up at Best Buy. "Come on," he urged.

Jazlyn followed him to the section with the laptops. She was floored when he stopped at the MacBooks. "Choose one."

"J—" No sooner than she started talking, she clamped her mouth shut. He had already warned her about the very thing that she was about to do. Jazlyn stole a glance at the dinner bill and couldn't believe that he spent fifty-five dollars on their meal, and he left the waitress a ten-dollar tip. Now, he was telling her to get one of the most expensive laptops in the store. Seeing the determined glare in his eye, she knew denying him would do no good, so she picked out the one that she wanted.

"Thank you so much. Really, I appreciate everything. This is the best birthday I've ever had," she confessed.

"I'm glad."

Jazlyn was full and sleepy and even more shocked when J2 pulled up at Walmart. "Be right back." He left the car running and got out of the car.

Jazlyn smiled and shook her head. She wasn't sure what he was up to, but just like that, he'd made her feel better than she had in a long time. Ten minutes later, she gasped as he came out of Walmart carrying a dozen roses and a birthday cake. "I swear you are doing the most, but thank you." She giggled.

"I just want to make sure you're good. You're an amazing person, Jazlyn, and you deserve to feel like you are. Got that?"

She simply nodded. His acts of kindness were doing nothing to extinguish her desire for him. If anything, her feelings were intensifying. Finally, he pulled up at her dorm room. "You can just bring my laptop to class tomorrow."

Not able to control herself, Jazlyn leaned over the armrest and placed a soft kiss on J2's cheek. "Thank you." After grabbing her things, she got out of the car and walked to her dorm with a smile on her face. She was officially in love.

"Them niggas not from round here. They from out of town, and they moving reckless as fuck. They all up through the south side. Niggas know that's your territory, but they not giving a fuck," J.J. reported to J2 about a problem that they encountered.

"How my money looking?" J2 asked as he pulled from his blunt.

"Money not fucked up *yet*. Their shit is watered down, bruh. Quality ain't shit, but that don't always stop niggas from switching sides. Money fucked up or not, they bold as hell to roll up in town and set up shop in our shit." J.J. was heated.

"Agreed. Let me think on it." If it was one thing J2 learned from his father, it was to not move based off emotions. When it came to his money, his life, and his freedom, every move he made needed to be calculated and meticulous. J2 sighed as Natori called him for the hundredth time. "I gotta get home, but we will definitely talk tomorrow." He stood up and gave his cousin dap before leaving.

The entire drive home, he replayed what Jazlyn confessed to him. J2 was still angry, but he knew there was nothing that he could do about it. Nothing except make Jazlyn feel special and appreciated. Despite his father being in the streets heavy, he had a home life that rivaled the Huxtables. His father always made sure they were spoiled, loved, and comfortable. He'd never seen struggle a day in his life. He couldn't fathom his parents doing anything foul to him. The way his father looked at him when he told him he wanted to hustle was one that J2 would never forget. Jules Baptiste wasn't afraid of shit, but he was scared of his son getting in the game. He was disappointed, scared, and pissed, but rather than let J2 jump in the water with sharks, he gave in and gave him the game. Unconditional love was what his father had for him. How a mother could pimp her own daughter was the weirdest and sickest shit in the world to J2.

Once he pulled up at his apartment, he knew he had to free his mind from thoughts of Jazlyn. He knew Natori was up and ready for war. Sure enough, when he walked inside, she was sitting on the couch pouting with her arms folded underneath her breasts. "Where the fuck have you been?" she barked, jumping up from the couch. "I have called you a hundred times."

"Natori, I'm not in the mood, alright. I run two got damn trap houses. I got niggas calling my phone every five minutes wanting dope. I got niggas calling my phone every five minutes 'cause the count fucked up, or fiends acting up, or niggas moving in on my blocks. I can't be everywhere at once, and the last thing I need is to come home to a nagging ass broad." When all else failed, he knew he could flip shit on Natori. She was one of the main beneficiaries of his street dealings. When he threw that in her face, she would back down every time. If Natori knew that he had really been with Jazlyn for the past few hours, she'd have a damn fit.

Just as he hoped she would, Natori backed down. "I'm sorry, J2. I just get worried. I didn't mean to come at you like that. It's just, damn, it only takes two seconds to send a text." Her whole demeanor changed.

J2's face softened. "It's all good. Come here." Not in the mood to fight, he pulled Natori into his arms. "You're right. It takes two seconds to send a text. I'll do better."

She looked up at him and placed a gentle kiss on his lips. "I missed you so much," she whispered into his mouth.

"When I get out the shower, you gon' suck this dick?"

"I'm going to suck the soul out that shit."

"Say no more." J2 broke the embrace and headed for the shower. He needed weed and some pussy. He hoped that would be enough to erase thoughts of Jazlyn from his mind for the night.

Chapter Nine

"This nigga," Lyric mumbled as she paced the floor in her bedroom. Not going to the doctor and attempting to get pain pills off the street was harder than she thought it would be. There wasn't any way to ask around about who had pills without putting people in her business. Lyric was aware that pills could become difficult to get and expensive, and that was why a lot of people turned to heroin. It was plentiful and cheaper.

Lyric didn't give a damn how hard pills got to find, she would never resort to shooting up heroin. It was getting late, and she needed the guy she was trying to cop from to call her back before Jules came upstairs. Her phone rang, and she damn near jumped out of her skin.

Lyric had gone more than seven hours without a pill and her skin was clammy and she felt jittery. "Hello?" she answered anxiously.

"Yeah. Sorry it took me so long. I got 'em though. Ten pills was all I could get."

"That's straight. Where you at?"

"Just leaving Triangle Mall. Can you meet me?"

"Yes. I'm on my way."

"You're on your way where?" Jules asked curiously stepping into the bedroom.

"Um, Natori can't find her key, and she needs to lock up the shop. I'll be right back."

She was lying. Lyric was walking around the room fast as hell, and she couldn't even look him in the eye. It was very rare that she lied to him, but Jules knew when she was lying. And he didn't like that shit. His wife had no reason to lie to him about anything. Unless, she was cheating, and Jules knew that Lyric knew better than that. She wasn't ready to die. No way.

"Oh yeah. Let me ride with you." He tested her.

Jules noticed the panicked look on Lyric's face when he suggested riding with her. "No, why would you do that? I'll only be gone for a few minutes. Stay home with Bella. I will be right back." Lyric walked over, kissed her husband on the lips, and scurried from the room.

Jules had half a mind to follow her. She was acting too weird for his liking. Bella was old enough to stay home alone, especially if they were going to come right back. There had to be a reason that she didn't want him to ride with her, and it had Jules furious. He hated to be lied to by anyone, but by someone he loved, that shit made his soul singe with anger. Lyric only had about an hour to get her ass back to the crib. Her shop was a good twenty minutes away, and he had to allow her the time to get there and back. However, the wheels in his head began to turn and play tricks on his mind. An hour was enough time to link up with a nigga. What if she didn't have to stop by the shop at all?

Jules headed downstairs to his bar. He needed a shot or something to calm his nerves. As he poured a shot of cognac, he thought about calling his son and seeing if Natori was actually at the shop. Having to call his son to verify his wife's story made him feel like a lame, and a lame was some shit Jules would never be. More afraid than looking like a lame, he was afraid that maybe his son would tell him that Natori was at the crib. It was one thing to have doubts, but to have proof that his wife had lied to him would for sure make him feel some type of way. Jules threw the shot back and immediately poured another. As he walked back up the stairs to prepare for a shower, he sipped his drink a little slower.

Everything with him and Lyric had been good lately. Cheating was just some shit that she wouldn't do, so maybe she was keeping some other kind of secret from him. Jules swallowed the rest of the liquor in his glass, walked into his master bathroom and stripped. Turning on some music, he tried to clear his mind as he slid back the glass shower door and stepped inside the spacious shower large enough to hold five adults comfortably. The hot water massaged his muscles and he grabbed the shampoo to wash his dreads. He washed them at least twice a week. They were wild and thick, but no one could ever truthfully say they were dirty. Once his dreads were clean, Jules washed his body, rinsed off and stepped from the shower. As he dried off, the bathroom door slowly opened, and Jules raised one eyebrow. Bella would never enter his bathroom without knocking. When he saw his wife enter the bathroom with a smile on her face, his body relaxed. She'd been gone less than an hour. Wherever she went, she couldn't have done too much dirt in such a short amount of time.

"Damn, I was hoping to get in with you." She smiled, no longer looking nervous or anxious.

Jules pulled his wife into his arms. "Word? There's always in the morning," he replied before kissing the tip of her nose.

"Well, I'm about to take my shower, and then we can have some fun."

"Sounds like a plan," Jules replied, smacking her on the ass. He'd been tripping for nothing.

"You gon' come out with me?" Tre spoke into Reign's ear. He'd talked her into driving three hours to Charlotte since he was performing at a club there. He had to leave Charlotte and shoot to New York, so he wouldn't have time to stop in Durham.

She'd done what she told herself she wouldn't. Start playing around with school. Once she left the club, she wouldn't get home until about five in the morning and she had a 10 am class. Reign hadn't missed any days in that class so far, and she told herself missing one day wouldn't be so bad, but to start missing classes for Tre was something that she didn't want to make a habit out of. When he called her saying how much he missed her though, she couldn't deny him. This famous ass nigga was really feeling her! It had been three weeks since their meeting, and he called her every day no matter where he was.

Reign looked up at him with wide eyes. "Come out on stage? No, it's got to about a thousand people in that crowd."

"So. You look fly as fuck. I want them to see my girl. Come on." The DJ announced Tre and he headed for the stage with his hand pulling Reign with him.

Her heart thumped in her chest. The willingness that Tre had to show her off stroked Reign's ego like shit. With what felt like all eyes on her, she was nervous as hell, but with the way the crowd was chanting and rocking, maybe they weren't that focused on her. Reign didn't want to look like a complete dufus, so she relaxed and swayed her hips to the beat of Tre's song. She half liked the attention and half didn't. When Tre took off his shirt, Reign damn near fainted. Tre's sexiness was off the charts. She wondered if they'd be able to get a quickie in before he had to go to the airport. Shit, she did drive all that way to see him.

There were females trying to grab his leg and all. The thirst was real, yet Reign stood in a spot that she hadn't even tried to get. After he did three songs, Tre thanked the crowd and then shocked the shit out of her when he said, "Shout out to my baby Reign for driving to kick it with me tonight." He then walked over to her and placed a kiss on her forehead in front of everyone. He then led her off the stage and said something to his security guard.

The security guard then followed them out to the bus and kept watch so they could in fact get a quickie in. Once they were done, Tre pulled some money from his pocket. "Here's your gas money from coming here. Call me as soon as you get on the road. I'm going to talk to you the whole way back, to make sure you get back safely."

Reign smiled. "Thank you." She took the thick wad from his hand and gave him a quick peck on the lips. She knew it was way more than what she spent on gas, but Jules had always told her that if a nigga fuck with you, he gon' always give you more than what you need. If her mother saw something that cost $300 Jules would give Lyric $700. That's how he'd always been. Even with Reign. If she needed fifty dollars for a field trip, he gave her a hundred.

Tre led Reign from the bus, walked her to her car, and then gave her a hug. Once he walked off, she squealed like a pig. She had that nigga.

Chapter Ten

"I really want my tits and my ass done," Reign told Jayla as she observed herself in her full-length mirror.

Jayla looked up from the magazine that she was flipping through. She spoke about plastic surgery often, but she'd never heard Reign speak about it. "Why you want your body done all of a sudden? Is it because of Tre?"

Reign stared at her reflection. "Kind of. I look like a lil' ass girl. I have no hips, no ass, no boobs. I legit look thirteen, bruh." She pouted.

Jayla shook her head. "And that nigga still shows you off proudly. Don't get surgery for no nigga, Reign."

Reign turned around to eye her cousin. "Says the chick that talks about getting surgery every day."

"Yes, but I been wanting surgery for me. Not a man. I can pull niggas just the way I am. I just don't like having this pouch. You, on the other hand, have always been mad confident. Don't let those fake body broads in the industry make you start doubting yourself."

Reign sat down on her bed without responding. Jayla seemed like a bit of a hypocrite, but she was right. She'd never considered surgery until she started fucking with Tre and seeing the kind of women that he was around on a daily basis. That shit kind of fucked with her no matter how confident she'd been in the past.

"Is he still coming tomorrow?" Jayla asked.

Reign smiled. "Yes. He's staying for three days. He made me promise not to tell anybody, so you can't have any company while he's here. No one can know that he's here." Tre wasn't hesitant to stay with Reign because when she sent him her address, he Googled the property. She lived in a nice ass gated community, and the rent on a two-bedroom was $1,400 a month.

Tre knew she lived in a very upscale neighborhood, and as long as no one knew he was there, he felt he'd be good. Reign didn't strike him as a cruddy broad that would try to set him up. He was going to be patient and let her finish school, and then he was going to convince her to move to Virginia. Tre had just purchased a six-bedroom, five-bathroom house that ran him 1.3 million dollars. Who would turn down the opportunity to live there with him? Tre knew that it was only a matter of time before Reign was doing whatever he wanted her to.

"I won't say anything. I'll even go stay at my dad's one night. Arianna is there alone. She didn't want to leave with Kymani."

Reign's face fell. "Damn, I hate that she left. I like Kymani. She's so sweet."

"Yeah. Shit, I love her. She's the only mother I've ever known, but you know how my dad is. I don't think they're going to fix it this time," Jayla stated with a solemn expression on her face.

"You sure you want to do this?" Arbrianna asked J.J. nervously. She was supposed to be calling to schedule her first doctor's appointment, but she wanted to make sure it was something that J.J. really wanted.

Regardless of how much money he had, he was a street nigga. His income wasn't traceable, so if he decided to shit on her, she couldn't exactly go take out child support on him. In the state of North Carolina, with no job, the most he'd be ordered to pay her was fifty dollars a month. If he didn't want the baby, he needed to let her know. There was no way that Arbrianna would be able to finish college and take care of a baby alone without his help. She only worked part-time. Her father paid her rent, and her job paid her utilities. She kept her hair and nails done courtesy of J.J. There was no way she could provide for a child on her own.

"What you mean am I sure? We talked about this."

"I know, but what about when Stacy isn't mad at you anymore? I don't have time for no flip-flopping type shit. I'm smart enough to know that if she takes you back, you'll go." Arbrianna pouted.

Even though she was in college, and her older sister had chosen not to attend college, Arbrianna always felt like she lived in Stacy's shadow. She had a job as a supervisor at a call center. Her record was squeaky clean, she took care of herself, and didn't have any children. Because of poor decisions, Arbrianna had been arrested twice in her life, and this was her second pregnancy. The first one was her sophomore year in high school, and her parents made her get an abortion. So, even though she was on the right path now and in school, Arbrianna still felt as if Stacy was that child that made her parents proud, while they held their breath and waited for Arbrianna to fuck up. Even a dope boy like Jacques couldn't leave her goody two shoes ass alone.

Upon hearing Arbrianna's words however, he sucked his teeth. "Chill, man. Stacy isn't my girl, and even if she was, I'm not choosing a female over my kid. You got me fucked up. Just make the appointment, and let me know when it is."

Jacques sat back and waited for Arbrianna to complete the call. He hated that he hurt Stacy the way that he did, but truth be told, he wasn't in love with her. He knew if he gave it some time, he'd be completely over their situation. She was a cool girl and all, but he couldn't continue fucking sisters, especially when one of them was carrying his seed. Stacy and Arbrianna were different, and they both had qualities that he liked. Arbrianna was a better fit for his lifestyle though, and she was about to be the mother of his child. That put her ahead of Stacy in the game, and he knew he had to leave Stacy all the way alone. He still didn't want a girlfriend, but as long as Arbrianna was carrying his child, she'd be at the top of the totem pole. She ended the call and looked over at him. "Friday at noon."

"Why you look so nervous, shawty? I told you I got you. You've never been nervous around me. Don't start now. I did some fucked up shit by getting at Stacy knowing she was your sister. I can be a fuck up for sho', but I fucks with you. And if you about to have my baby, you damn sure got to know I'm not fin to play 'bout you. Got it?" He pulled her into his arms.

Arbrianna simply nodded. She didn't even know why she stayed after J.J. fucked Stacy. For the same reason that heroin addicts shoot up, even when they knew the poison they were injecting into their veins could be the death of them. The euphoria that they felt after they got high was worth the risk to them, and that's how she felt about J.J. Call her dumb or whatever, but he made her high. A baby wasn't in her plans, but she sucked at remembering to take her pills, and now here they were. As long as he was willing to step up to the plate, she felt like everything would be okay. J.J. kissed her on the lips, letting his mouth linger on hers. His phone rang, and he broke the kiss with a sigh.

"Yo," he answered. "What?" he asked and took his arms from

around Arbrianna as he sat up. "Is he good?" J.J. listened intently for five seconds before responding. "I'm on my way. Clean that shit up."

"Everything okay?" Arbrianna asked as J.J. stood up.

"Hell nah. The spot in Durham just got hit, and Kareem is in the hospital. I'll be back."

Arbrianna watched as he collected his things and left her apartment abruptly. Even if he was willing to step up to the plate financially, she would always have to worry about whether or not J.J. would leave the house one day and never make it back home. When a man chose to deal drugs, that was a very real possibility. One that had her questioning whether or not she really wanted to have this baby.

Chapter Eleven

"You know it ain't nothing out here in these streets though, bruh. You really want to walk away from Kymani?" Jules asked his brother. They were at Jacques' club having a drink, and Jules was trying to pick his brother's brain. He knew that Jacques could be stubborn as hell and that maybe he was just mad at Kymani and being overly dramatic.

Jacques threw back his shot of vodka. "It's not even about me being out here looking for anything. Since Kymani left, I haven't fucked anything. I just been chilling, especially since Arianna is at the crib. I really can't explain it. Like, I got love for Kymani, but I don't think I'm in love with her anymore. Forcing that shit is no good for anybody. I've never loved anyone the way that I loved Brooke. Kymani came along, and she took away my pain, but I just don't know, man. Take you and Lyric. Do you love her the same now as you did ten years ago?"

Jules frowned up his face. "Hell nah. I love her ass way more than that. The love I have for Lyric is strong as fuck. As time goes by, it gets even stronger. Years ago, that shit scared me. I was like gah damn, did this broad put roots on me? I love her ass so much it's scary. Dangerous even, 'cause I'll murder 'bout her quick as hell." Jules' eyes darkened at even the hypothetical thought of someone bothering Lyric.

"That's exactly my point, bruh. My shit with Kymani hasn't gotten stronger. Some days, it feels like that shit damn near disappeared. I can't settle, bruh. If my heart isn't all the way in it, I gotta go. Weird shit is, I wasn't even thinking of leaving 'til she forced me to tell the truth about how I felt. I was content just being there faking it. It wasn't all bad, and I don't hate Kymani. It's just if I'm being honest, marriage isn't for me anymore, and if it's not 'cause I want to fuck mad hoes, then I don't even know what the deal is, big bruh." Jacques honestly looked confused.

Jules reached for the vodka bottle. "Sometimes, we just outgrow people, Jac. It is what it is. I hate that Kymani got hurt because she's family. But if that's not where you want to be, you did the right thing by setting her free. Now on to other matters." Jules face darkened slightly. "You heard about the spot in Durham getting shot up? I know what comes with the game, but I get nervous every time I hear about gunplay." Jules' hand tightened around the glass in his hand. "I really wish J2 would get over this lil' street addiction bullshit."

Jacques let out a chuckle. "Same way we got over it after how long in the game? I don't like it either, bruh, but them lil' niggas gon' do what they wanna do. It doesn't really excite me either, but all we can do is support them. And by support, I mean if they need me to strap up and ride, I'm with the shits," Jacques retorted with a gleam in his eyes.

"Yeah, well J2 is going to be mad at me for not letting him handle it on his own, but I got the drop on one of the lil' niggas. The ring leader. Nigga from Baltimore thought he was gon' come to town and take shit over. He 'bout to find out he stepped into the wrong hood," Jules stated with an evil smirk on his face, causing Jacques to smile. The brothers had caused a lot of hell on earth, but for their children, they'd dance with the devil himself.

"You been on that damn phone for thirty minutes. Put that shit down," Tre stated before leaning over and easing his tongue into Reign's mouth.

After a succulent kiss, their lips separated, and she smiled. "I know. It's a habit. What's up? What you want to do?" she asked, putting the phone down beside her on the bed.

"Get up, and get dressed. I got somebody stopping by."

Reign raised an eyebrow in confusion. This man, the one that was so adamant about her not having any company at her crib while he was there, had someone coming over. Normally, after being holed up inside for more than a day, Reign would start to go crazy, but she'd enjoyed the past two days with Tre. They shut themselves off from the world and got to know each other. When they weren't talking, they were having sex. When they weren't having sex, they were eating and watching movies. Reign had cooked for him twice, and the other times, they ordered take out. She was still unsure about his plans for her, but for every day that passed, Reign was falling harder for Tre da Don. He seemed so genuine and sincere, and she felt like he really liked her. Or at least that's how he made her feel. She knew that her father and brother were skeptical about it, but Reign was grown. She had to live her own life and make her own mistakes. Plus, what if they got together, and he really did do right by her?

"Who?" she asked, sitting up.

Tre got up and slipped some basketball shorts on over his Versace boxer briefs. "It's a surprise. Hurry up, 'cause ain't nobody coming in here with you dressed like that."

All Reign had on was an Ethika sports bra and some matching boxer briefs. In the tight material, her butt sat up and looked nice and juicy. It gave the illusion that she was working with a little bit more than she actually was. Deciding just to trust him, Reign stood up and walked over to her dresser. After pulling out some black leggings, she grabbed her brush and began to do her hair. Her eyes bounced back and forth from her reflection to Tre's muscular frame. He stood in the middle of her bedroom, scrolling through his phone with intensity etched onto his face. He looked like he was really concentrating on something, and that made Reign smile. Had anyone told her a month ago that she'd be shut up in the apartment for three whole days cuddling with and fucking Tre da Don, she would have had a good hearty laugh at the foolishness. Now, she felt like she was borderline in love with his ass.

After brushing her long weave, Reign tied a scarf around the top of her head, to make sure her edges stayed laid. Once she was done with that, she headed over to make her bed and the doorbell rang. She looked up at Tre curiously, and he simply smiled. "That's my people. Come on."

She followed him through the living room like it was his apartment. Once he opened the door, Reign's eyes fell on a short man that looked to be of maybe Iranian descent. He carried a large briefcase in his hand. Dude was dressed in Gucci from head to toe and the watch on his wrist damn near blinded Reign.

"My man Adu." Tre grinned giving him dap. He then turned to look at Reign. "This is my jeweler, Adu. This is my baby Reign."

Reign blushed at being presented as his baby. "Hi." She smiled bashfully.

Adu stepped inside and shut the door behind him. He didn't even wait for Tre to lock it; he locked it himself. In his briefcase was over a million dollars' worth of jewelry. Adu was cautious as fuck at all times. "She has to be a special lady. I've never been summoned to you while you were with a female."

"She is special. Have a seat."

Reign looked on curiously as Adu walked over to the couch and opened his briefcase. "I decided to do a lil' shopping, so my man came all the way from Virginia for me. He knows when I call him I'm trying to spend bread. Pick out anything you want," Tre stated to Reign, causing her to almost choke on her tongue.

She had plenty of expensive pieces, but they'd all been purchased by her dad. Jules wouldn't allow Reign to date street niggas, so most of the guys she had dated in the past were broke. Their parents may have had a lil' bread, and they drove nice cars and took her to nice places, but they weren't holding for real. The most a guy had ever spent on her was when she was a senior in high school, and her ex paid $275 for her class ring. Now she was eyeing all kinds of diamonds, and Tre was telling her to get whatever she wanted. Reign was ecstatic as hell, but she tried to remain cool on the outside. She walked closer to the briefcase and eyed everything inside.

"Everything is so pretty." She gushed as Tre picked up a watch and inspected it. As he talked with Adu, she picked up a ring. It was a simple ring made like a wedding band, but it was filled with diamonds. She finally decided that's what she wanted. Of course, she wouldn't wear it on her ring finger. Reign slipped the ring onto her pointer finger and held her hand out to admire the way that the diamonds gleamed.

"Can I get this one?"

Tre looked up and glanced at her finger. "Yeah, bae. I told you, you can get whatever you want. What's the tag on that one Adu?"

"For anybody else, twelve grand, but for you, I will let it go for nine."

"Aight, that's what's up."

Reign headed for her room, smiling so wide her face damn near hurt. The trolls had been back at it something vicious on social media, and now she was going to really give them a reason to hate her ass. She wasn't going to snap Tre or his jeweler at her apartment, but she did turn on some Gucci and flex for the Snapchat and Instagram. When she was trying to be reserved and humble, bitches were running their mouths anyway. So now, she was about to turn up for them. She made several videos, flexing her new ring in them all. It was official, if Tre was spending that kind of money on jewelry for her, then he wasn't planning on going anywhere.

An hour later, Adu was leaving. Tre had spent too much damn money with him, but it was his, he earned it. Tre was at the point in his career where he was getting 40k for a show and 25k for walk throughs at the clubs. He did at least eight walk throughs a month, so Tre was getting $200,000 a month *just* from showing up at the clubs. He didn't even always perform when he went. He just had to be there. When the crowd was showing him mad love, he'd perform anyway though and give them a good show. In a few cities he went to, the goons came out extra hard. Dumb ass niggas would pay all that money to get in the club and then mean mug all night and act mad that Tre was there. At one show, a nigga even threw a bottle on stage at him, and Tre had his security toss the nigga out. At shows like that, he just stood in VIP and gritted back. He found it funny that he was being paid 25k, and niggas showed up just to hate and act tough.

"I'm lowkey sad tomorrow is my last day with you." Tre hugged Reign tight after Adu left.

She was no longer trying to play hard and fight her feelings. He spent all of the time he could with her, so she had to be the only woman he was interested in. Reign wasn't going to let doubt ruin this thing for her. Her mother was a firecracker, but she was always submissive when it came to Jules because he deserved it. Reign wasn't going to try to play the situation cool and seem uninterested. If he was a regular guy, maybe, but Tre was far from regular.

"Me too, but wherever you are next weekend, I'll fly to you. I can do all my work this week and be ahead. As long as I have my work turned in, it won't hurt me to miss my Friday classes. In fact, I can fly out Thursday night."

Tre smiled. "Word? I'll be in New York Thursday, and then I leave

Friday night headed back to VA. I'll get you a ticket to New York and then one to VA."

"Sounds like a plan." Reign smiled. "Aye, if people keep seeing us together, they're going to think I'm your girlfriend."

Tre stared her in the eyes with the most serious look that he could muster. "You are my girlfriend."

Chapter Twelve

"J2, I know that's you." She chuckled when someone walked up behind her and covered her eyes with their hand. She smelled him. That familiar and intoxicating scent. It seemed as if J2 wore a different fragrance every day, but each and every one of them had been engraved into Jazlyn's memory. She lived for those smells.

He removed his hand and smiled. "What you got going on?" he asked as he moved into her view.

"About to go back to my dorm."

J2 frowned up his face. "That's all you ever do. Yo' life got to be boring as fuck, my nigga."

Jazlyn giggled. "It really is." She was used to her routine, and on this day, it didn't even bother her. Ever since J2 took her out for her birthday, she'd been happy. There had been no sad days, and Jazlyn prayed that it stayed that way. "I have something for you though," she said shyly.

J2 looked at her curiously. "For me? What?"

"It's in my dorm room. Follow me."

J2 knew he'd be pushing it if he took her out to the movies. He really just felt bad for her though. She really had no social life, and shorty damn sure wasn't ugly. She was just to herself, and that made it so she didn't have many friends. Jazlyn wasn't into the wild shit a lot of other college students were into, so they looked past her altogether. J2 hated that for her. Anxious to see what she had for him, he followed her into her dorm room. As soon as he entered, the smell of cinnamon smacked him in the face.

"I made you an apple cobbler." She let him taste her apple cobbler once, and he was hooked from there.

The ways his eyes lit up as she passed him the container made him smile. "Damn that's what's up Jaz. A nigga gon' kill this tonight. I appreciate that."

"It's no problem. The least I can do. Especially after you took me out."

"That was nothing. I eat out damn near every day."

For a moment, Jazlyn wondered what it would be like to have money to blow. To have a loving family and people that wanted to be him everywhere he went. People either wanted to be him or be with him. Jazlyn assumed that to have a life like that was an awesome feeling. A feeling that she would probably never know. J2's voice interrupted her thoughts.

"Where is your roommate? Shorty moved out, didn't she? You don't have anyone that you could go watch a movie with or go out to eat with? I'll pay for the both of you. I would take you but..." his voice trailed off. Jazlyn knew he couldn't take her out in public like that because he had a girlfriend. If someone saw them and it got back to Natori, she'd be pissed.

It made Jazlyn feel good that J2 cared so much about her. On one hand, it almost made her feel pathetic, but the gesture meant a lot to her. She did have someone she could invite. A girl by the name of

Chyna that was in her African-American studies class. Just as she opened her mouth to speak, J2 interrupted her. "And it has to be a female. I'm not paying for you to go out with no nigga."

Jazlyn smiled. "Of course not. I can ask Chyna if she wants to go out to eat. Maybe we can stop by that new Hookah lounge. I want to know what the fascination is."

J2 raised his eyebrows. "Look at you. Aight, bet. See if shorty wanna go. You think two hundred dollars is enough?"

Jazlyn's mouth fell open. His extravagance baffled her. "Yes, that's more than enough."

"Cool." J2 pulled money from his pocket and placed it on her dresser. He really was happy to see that after everything that she confessed to him that she'd been smiling lately. Every time he thought about what she'd gone through, he got mad all over again.

"You really good? Like for real?" he asked her.

"Jules Baptiste Junior, I am fine."

A crooked smile graced his face. "Watch that shit. Nobody call me that but my moms." He lowkey liked it when she said it though. "I'm 'bout to get out of here. Thanks for the cobbler." Even though he announced his departure, J2 didn't move. His gaze was locked with Jazlyn's, and he wasn't sure what was happening.

She'd always been cute to him, but he never had sexual urges around her. It made him feel almost uncomfortable to be lusting after her after she told him what happened to her when she was a child, but the attraction at that moment was strong as fuck. Jazlyn felt it too. The way he was looking at her didn't make her feel dirty, and it didn't make her feel nervous, she welcomed the sexual energy hanging in the air. When she hit fifteen, something went off in her, and she went through a hoe phase, which she didn't know at the time wasn't uncommon in rape victims. She had sex with six guys over the course of nine months before the reality of what she was doing smacked her in the face, and she became disgusted with herself. Jazlyn hadn't had sex since then and that was three years ago. But she wanted J2 bad as fuck, and he seemed to feel the same way about her.

Just when he was about to make himself leave, Jazlyn stepped closer to him, letting him know that she wanted it just as bad as he did.

She may have been wrong, but at that time, she didn't care about him having a girlfriend. All she cared about was how he treated her and how he made her feel. Guys with way less money and status than him had been rude and disrespectful to her countless times, but this one man that damn near everybody worshipped treated her like a queen. He was never cocky, arrogant, or rude to her. He never acted like she should bow down to him, and he was the sweetest guy she'd ever had the pleasure of knowing. She was almost embarrassed that she'd baked him a cobbler like some little girl. She wanted to give him something far greater.

When Jazlyn took a step towards him, that was all the motivation that J2 needed. He closed the space in between them and placed his lips on hers. They engaged in an erotic tongue kiss that had Jazlyn pulling his shirt over his head. She prayed that he wouldn't remember his girlfriend and stop her, because that rejection would embarrass the fuck out of her. J2 had no plans of stopping though. In fact, he was glad that despite having a girlfriend, something told him to always keep a condom in his wallet.

J2 softly sucked the flesh of Jazlyn's neck as he helped her to remove her clothes. He damn sure wasn't thinking about right or wrong. Once she was completely naked, he had to avoid looking at her legs. Seeing the scars would make him angry all over again and kill the mood. Jazlyn was self-conscious about them, so she headed over to the bed and wasted no time getting underneath the covers. It wasn't until the condom was on J2's dick and his body was covering hers that he suddenly had a conscience. No matter how attracted to her he was, when he walked out of that dorm room, he would have to go home to Natori. He wasn't trying to treat Jazlyn like some side chick, but that's just what it was. If them having sex was going to make her feel some type of way, then he'd have to muster enough willpower to stop himself from going there with her.

"Jazlyn, I want this, but you do know that I can't just go home and leave Natori? If this is going to complicate things then…" His voice trailed off, and she smiled.

"It's fine, Jules. In all honesty, I've wanted this for a minute. If I only have it one time, that's fine," she replied in a small voice, shocking him.

J2 slowly entered Jazlyn's tight opening. He could tell that sex definitely wasn't something that she had a lot of. She sucked in a breath, and J2 looked at her with a face full of concern. Placing his lips on hers, he kissed her to relax her and then pushed himself the rest of the way in. Jazlyn immediately placed her palms on his back and held him close to her as he moved in and out of her. It didn't hurt at all, and J2 felt so good. The way he was being so gentle with her, the way his cologne was filling her nostrils, it was all euphoric. With every stroke, she got wetter and Jazlyn lifted her legs some so he could go deeper in her. Hearing him moan softly in her ear did something to her and her clitoris started throbbing. No way would she be satisfied with doing this only one time, but he did have a girl, and Jazlyn couldn't ignore that.

Jazlyn moaned and played in his dreads as he increased his pace just a little. By the time his tongue swirled over her nipple, Jazlyn's stomach tightened, and she felt the urge to pee. She'd never had an orgasm before. After she went through her hoe phase, she became ashamed of her actions and refused to even masturbate. She didn't want to be the girl that let poor decisions and sex take control of her life. She was still human, so of course she got terribly horny, but she always pushed through it. Only her strong attraction to J2 and the way he treated her made her want to go there with him. He felt so good inside of her that the last thing she wanted to do was stop him, but it would be super embarrassing to pee on him.

"Ju—" Before she could call his name, he sped up the pace, and she gasped as a feeling so powerful rocked through her core that she moaned way louder than she intended to. Her body trembled, and her pussy contracted on his dick as she felt like an earthquake had just taken place inside of her body. If that's what an orgasm was, she could see why some people chased sex like a drug addict chasing a high.

Her pussy got creamy and wetter as J2 gently bit her neck, and her body came down from the orgasmic high. "Can I hit it from the back?" he whispered in her ear.

She nodded, and they changed positions. Jazlyn's back arched as he slid into her from behind. She grabbed a fistful of sheets and bit the pillow as he plowed in and out of her. His grunts were so sexy to her, and she felt like she was going to cum again. J2 smacked her on the ass and Jazlyn screamed into the pillow. God why did he feel so good? When he reached around her and stroked her clit, that was it. Jazlyn came once again and that time he was right behind her. J2 exploded into the condom with a deep moan and he and Jazlyn collapsed onto the bed. He really couldn't believe that he'd just had sex with Jazlyn.

Jazlyn's chest heaved up and down, and she had no regrets. Sleeping with J2 in her mind, was one of the best decisions that she ever made. Yes, he belonged to someone else, and yes, some may view her as stupid for giving him her body, but the way he made her feel. Wanted. That was something that she had been chasing her entire life. She would sleep with him again and again if he allowed it. She had nothing against Natori, and she didn't want to hurt Natori, but this was deeper than her. J2 filled a void in her life that she'd been missing since a child. Not even the throbbing between her legs was enough to make her feel bad. Jazlyn stood up to go pee and when she wiped, she saw blood on the tissue, but she knew that was normal. It had been a very long time since she had sex, and J2 was pretty blessed in the size department. When she left the bathroom, he was sitting on the edge of her bed.

"I have to get going."

It was cute to her the way he handled her, like she was so delicate. She knew he couldn't stay. She didn't expect him to. "Okay. Don't forget your cobbler."

J2 got dressed, grabbed his dessert, gave her a hug, and left. Jazlyn covered her mouth with her hand and giggled. She had sex with Jules Baptiste Junior, and she liked it.

Chapter Thirteen

"What's this about?" J2 asked his dad curiously as he entered the old farm house that his dad asked him and J.J. to come to.

Jules backed up slightly allowing his son enough room to pass through. "You'll see soon enough," was his reply as he closed the door back and locked it.

Jules then led his son through an empty living room into the kitchen. What he saw in the kitchen astonished him. A short dark-skinned was slumped down in a metal folding chair. He'd been beaten so badly that he couldn't even sit up straight. In the kitchen, standing quiet as church mice, were J.J., Jacques, and Jules' protégé Bishop. When Jules retired from the game, he handed everything over to Bishop, including his clientele and his connect. One thing about the drug game though, it's lucrative as fuck. There are enough people with addictions for all the dope boys to eat. Well, the dope boys that were good at what they did. On top of that, Bishop dabbled in coke. J2's specialty was heroin. Two very different drugs but two very profitable hustles. When Jules put his son up on game, he was careful not to step on Bishop's toes out of respect for the loyalty that Bishop had always given him.

"Who is this?" J2 asked looking over at his father.

Jules answered while never taking his eyes off his victim. "Philly. The nigga that thought he was going to come in and take over your blocks. Him and his little minions really thought they had what it took to go to war with the Baptiste boys."

Years ago, Jules had done the same thing. He came from Miami with a crew of niggas and took over blocks, but the difference between him and Philly was that he was built for that shit. Jules and his crew came to town and shut shit down. Philly had bitten off way more than he could chew.

J2 looked at his father in disbelief. He didn't even know his father knew about his problem. A problem that he was handling, or so he thought he was. "How did you end up with this nigga?"

Jules smirked. "The oldest trick in the book. Nigga came to town with three other niggas and a bitch. The bitch, Rasheeda is like half these hoes out here. Disloyal. I put my man Bishop on her, and he tried to holla at her. Shorty folded too damn quick. I got him to hit her up on some wanting to chill type shit. He told her that he wanted her to himself for a few hours and asked if she could get away from her nigga. Shorty gave up dude's entire location. Ready to give that pussy up, she didn't even know she was signing her nigga's death certificate. He had his niggas touch ours, and Kareem got hit, so now it's time for vengeance." Jules snarled.

His father had handed him Philly's head on a platter, but J2 had the shit under control. He was going to make a move on him when he wanted to. His father just took it upon himself to step in and damn near handle everything for him. In taking over his father's legacy, he wanted to make his own waves, not live in his dad's shadow. J2 chose his words carefully, not wanting to sound like a kid having a tantrum.

"I had this under control though. You not even in the streets no more. Why would you involve yourself in this? If Bishop had beef, would you insert yourself in it?" he asked respectfully.

Jules flicked the tip of his nose. "Bishop isn't my son. You got damn right, I'm gon' be by ya side inserting myself into any damn thing that I see fit. You want to be a boss and earn your stripes, do that shit," Jules stated as he handed him a brand-new Glock. He knew J2 would be pissed, but he didn't give a damn. As long as he was breathing, he would always ride for his son.

If J2 took too long to make a move, he would be giving Philly time to make connections, get his money up, calculate moves, etc. Time wasn't of the essence, so he stepped in and handled the shit for him. He wasn't going to tell J2 where he went wrong though, not in front of everyone. They would have a private conversation later. Not in the mood for anymore small talk, J2 caressed the trigger of the gun. He aimed it at Philly and sent a bullet slamming into the man's head. Blood and brain matter splattered onto the wall and Jules looked over at J.J.

"Y'all get rid of this nigga's body." He was willing to help out every now and then, but if his son and his nephew wanted to be 'bout that life, some shit he was going to leave to them.

"Damn, have you had any days off?" Kymani's co-worker Greg asked as he approached her at the nurse's station.

Kymani was going over charts with a weary look on her face. It was her thirteenth day in a row at work. Most days, she worked twelve-hour shifts, but on this day, she was helping the hospital because they were short staffed, so she was only doing eight. She gave him a tired smile. "Not lately, but that will change soon. I will be off in three more days, and I just put in for a week off next month. I'm going to Los Angeles."

"Sounds nice," he said, looking down at her hand to see that her ring was still missing. Greg had been admiring Kymani from afar for almost a year, but unlike the other married women that worked at the hospital, she never flirted with her male co-workers, and he had the feeling that she wasn't one to cheat on her husband. Jacques was well-known around the hospital, and Greg could tell that even though Kymani talked about her husband's businesses, he was a thug to the T. Greg didn't want those problems.

It had been almost a month though, and her finger was still bare. She was working herself to death, and she rarely smiled anymore. Greg smelled trouble in paradise. He didn't want to be a rebound though, so he decided to just play it by ear.

"Family vacation?" he probed.

Kymani let out a sarcastic laugh. "Nope. I don't have much of a family these days. I'm going alone to try and regroup and get my head right."

"Nothing wrong with that at all, but be careful all the way out in L.A. alone."

"I will. I'm a big girl." Kymani gave Greg a tense smile.

"I believe you. I still want you to be careful."

He walked away, and Kymani took a deep breath. These days, work was the only thing keeping her sane. She went home alone to an empty, quiet house. She wasn't mad at her daughter or trying to punish her, but Kymani was going through. She texted Arianna every day, but since she made it clear that she wanted to stay with her dad, Kymani didn't go see her or ask her to come over. She'd never felt so alone in her life. Lyric called to check on her daily, but that did nothing to brighten Kymani's mood. She dedicated her life to Jacques. Gave him her heart, and he stepped on it. She wasn't sure what she was going to California to do, but she knew that she needed to get away from North Carolina. Maybe for good. The pay for traveling nurses was awesome. Even though she was grieving the demise of her marriage, Kymani refused to just curl up in a ball and die. Work was a distraction for her, but it was also a blessing to her bank account. Jacques offered to pay her bills, and she was damn sure going to take him up on that offer. Fuck being independent and telling him that she didn't need his money. That was the least his ass could do. Every month that he put money in her account, she was going to spend that shit.

The hotel room that she booked in Los Angeles was running her $1,500 for five nights. She was going to go and have the time of her life. Kymani was going to put herself first for a change, and that was very scary for her. It took her a lot of crying and thinking to come to the conclusion that Jacques was absolutely wrong for cheating on her. It was a tough decision for her to choose between walking away from her marriage and forgiving him. She forgave him, but her forgiveness came with conditions. For years, she did accuse him of lying and cheating when he wasn't doing anything. She finally took the drastic measures to go to a voodoo priestess, and she got her truth. An ugly truth that ripped her heart from her chest. But Jacques was right. If he didn't want to be married, he shouldn't be. What that taught Kymani was that you can be a good wife, a good homemaker, a good mother, and none of it will matter if your significant other isn't in love with you the way they should be. Her self-esteem wasn't so low that she wanted Jacques to remain with her out of guilt, so she was letting the marriage go. They'd both done wrong, and now it was time for her to start a new chapter of her life.

At this time, she wasn't interested in dating or bringing another man into her life. Kymani was going to focus on falling in love with herself so that hopefully issues like this would not be a problem in the future. Kymani's main goal was to fall in love with herself. Fuck her marriage. It had run its course.

On the other side of town, Jacques was heading into the mall. Jayla's birthday was coming up, and she had shown him a few pairs of shoes that he wanted. His main focus was making his kids happy, even the ones that were grown. Some days, he woke up feeling like dirt, but what was he supposed to do? He and Kymani had a good run, and it was his hope that one day they could even be friends. But it was what it was. He'd seen people fall out of love and force themselves to stay together because of the years they put in or the kids they had. Jacques refused to be that guy.

"Jacques? Hey." He turned around at the sound of the familiar voice, and when his eyes made contact with hers, he couldn't believe it.

He hadn't seen her in years. "Rella? What's good?"

Chapter Fourteen

Lyric was at the shop doing her client's hair, and she was once again sweating bullets. She rushed out of the house and left her phone on the charger. By the time she realized her mistake, she had been driving for five minutes. Turning around would have made her late, and her client had to get started on time because she was coming in before work. Reign only did the hair of four clients that had been coming to her for years. They swore that no one but Lyric could touch their hair. They tipped her gladly after each visit because they knew she was pretty much retired from doing hair. She was supposed to meet up with Jason, and he'd probably been calling her phone. Lyric knew that it was a bad thing that she couldn't go more than seven or eight hours without a pill before she started having nasty withdrawal symptoms.

She knew exactly what an addict was, but she couldn't stop cold turkey. When her body needed pain pills, it did things that made her extremely uncomfortable. Her skin grew clammy and she broke out in cold sweats. Her stomach would cramp, and she'd feel sick on the stomach. When Lyric needed pain pills, she was cranky and irritable. She told herself that after a few more weeks, she'd talk to Kymani. Maybe there was something that she could do to wean herself off the pills rather than quitting cold turkey.

"Hey, Mrs. Baptiste," Natori called out as she entered the shop.

Lyric just gave her a smile. She was starting to feel like shit, and she needed to hurry up and get to her phone. Natori noticed the look on her face. "You okay, ma?"

Lyric resisted the urge to roll her eyes, and she instantly knew that her attitude was about to be on ten if she didn't get out of that shop. When Natori didn't call her Mrs. Baptiste, she called her ma, and Lyric felt that was a bit presumptuous of her. She was J2's first serious girl-friend, and he was young. Lyric didn't understand why Natori felt that J2 would marry her, but whatever helped her to sleep at night.

"Yeah, I'm fine. My stomach is just cramping a little bit."

Conversation carried on around her from everyone in the shop, and Lyric busied herself with finishing up her client's hair. After another fifteen minutes, she was done. Breathing a sigh of relief as she waited for her client to pay her, Lyric knew that in less than thirty minutes, she would be home and she could call Jason and find out where to meet him.

Jules exited his gym and headed upstairs to take a shower. He didn't care if Lyric only did hair once a week and only did one head when she did go to work, on the days that she worked, Jules always took her and Bella out for dinner. He told Lyric that she never had to come home from work and cook. He was going to take a shower so as soon as Bella got off the bus, they'd be ready to head out. His eyebrows dipped low when he heard vibrating and buzzing. After searching the room with his eyes, he found Lyric's cell phone on the nightstand charging. She must have forgotten it. Walking over to the nightstand, he absent-mindedly picked the phone up and disconnected it from the charger. If she wasn't home by the time he got out of the shower, he would take it to her. Jules did a double take at the name on the screen. Jason? Why the fuck was a dude named Jason calling his wife's phone? Jules had never been an insecure guy, but certain shit he just didn't play about.

"Yo?" He barked into the phone after answering.

"Um, is Lyric around?"

Jules could tell that the guy on the other end of the phone was white. He didn't care though. White or black, he could get fucked up. "Nah, she's not. Why are you calling my wife?"

Jason began to stutter. "Uh, s-she called me. I just get her pills whenever she needs them."

Jules' face contorted into a frown. Lyric had a doctor that she got pills from. "How often does my wife get pills from you? And what kind?"

Jason knew he'd fucked up. Usually, his loyalty was with his customers, but he knew Jules didn't play. He wasn't trying to come up missing over Lyric's habits. "She just started hitting me up again recently. I hadn't heard from her in months, but for the past few weeks, she hits me up pretty often. I get her about twenty Percs every ten days. If I can't get Percs, I get Lortabs."

Jules clenched his jaws together. He was so heated the vein in his neck was straining against his skin looking like it was about to pop out. "Listen to me, homeboy. I don't care what Lyric calls you wanting. You are not to serve her. She's cut off. If you give her any pills, and I find out, we got problems, my G. Aight?"

"I got you. I'll block her number right now, dude."

Jules ended the call furious as hell. He searched through Lyric's phone until he found her doctor's number. When the receptionist answered, he told her to have the doctor to call him ASAP. Just as he was getting off the phone, Lyric entered the bedroom. "Hey, babe. My phone was ringing?" She tried to act normal all the while praying that Jason hadn't called.

Lyric looked at his wife with anger in his eyes. He'd struggled with addiction, so a part of him wanted to feel sorry for her, but how was his wife a whole pill head, and he didn't know it?

"Yeah, Jason called. And I let him know that you're cut off. He's not to serve you anymore. Lyric, you need help, ma."

Lyric's blood boiled. She was already sweating, but at the moment, she literally felt hot. "You told him what? You had no fucking right to do that! I need those pills."

Jules shook his head. "Bae, you sound like a whole fiend right now. You have a doctor. Why are you buying pills off the street? That shit is dangerous. I called your doctor too though. You're addicted to them joints, and we're going to get them out of your system."

"We?" Lyric screeched. "You have some fucking nerve! Just because you were once addicted to coke, doesn't mean that everyone is an addict, Jules. I don't say shit about you smoking five blunts a day." Lyric was on the verge of tears.

Jules was no longer angry. Instead, his eyes held pity for his wife. Lyric was always so strong-willed and determined. To see something have such a hold over her damn near brought him to tears, but he had to be strong for his wife. Addiction was real, and he would be damned if he stood by and watched his wife spiral out of control. He wasn't judging her, he was focused on helping her. She was mad defensive, about to cry over some pills. It was bad, and he was ashamed of himself for not noticing sooner. When Jules spoke to his wife, he kept his tone low and his voice soft.

"Babe, we can get you some help. It'll be okay. You strong as shit, Lyric. This shit is nothing. Small thing to a giant, ma."

Lyric didn't want to hear words of encouragement. She didn't want to be comforted by Jules She wanted pills. She was hot and sweaty, and she felt lightheaded. The one thing that would make her feel better, Jules had ruined it for her. Lyric snatched her phone from Jules and rushed from the house. She didn't know where to go get pills, but she had to at least try. Her body felt as if it was about to shut down on her. It wasn't a good feeling at all. Add in the fact that Jules had busted her, and Lyric was devastated. It wouldn't be impossible for her to keep using pills under Jules' nose, but using would be extremely difficult since he'd put everybody in her business. Tears streamed down Lyric's face as she got in her car. She wasn't even sure of where she was going, but she had to get the hell away from there.

"I don't know." Reign's voice trailed off. "My dad is getting kind of irritated that I'm never around anymore. I haven't visited him and my mom in weeks. When I'm not with you, I'm trying to catch up on homework." Reign and Tre had only been on the phone for thirty minutes, and he was already becoming agitated with her.

Yeah, Reign was in college, but shorty was almost twenty-two years old. The hold that her parents had on her was frustrating. Tre had to remind himself that he wanted a chick that came from money, so it would do him no good to go find a broad with no goals and no ambition, just so she could be by his side every day. It was hard having a woman that had restrictions on when she could get to him while everywhere he went damn near, women were throwing themselves at him. Just that morning at the airport, one of the broads from TSA slid him her number. Tre was a hot commodity in the streets, yet Reign cared more about pleasing her father than him.

He sucked his teeth, not even bothering to hide his agitation. "Reign, you not twelve, shawty. You a grown ass woman. I get that your father loves you, but he can't hold your hand for the rest of your life. I'm not just anybody. I'm yo' nigga." He huffed into the phone.

Reign chewed on her bottom lip. She and Tre had moved extremely fast. Yes, they spent hours sometimes on the phone, and they learned a lot about each other when he was at her apartment for those three days, but you don't truly know someone until you've been around them. That's the one thing her and Tre weren't able to do and that was to be around each other a lot. Reign did care about pleasing her father, but Tre was right. She was grown, and Jules would just have to get over it. It wasn't like it had been months since she'd visited her parents. It had only been a few weeks. Tre was having a party at his house, and he wanted his woman there. She was sure she could get her mother to understand, and then she could calm Jules down. No one could tame Jules like her mother could.

Before Reign could tell Tre she would come, his manager instructed him that he was about to go on air, and he had to get in the room with the radio hosts. "I'll hit you back." Tre ended the call abruptly, voice full of attitude.

Reign frowned up her face, ready to text him and curse him out, but she didn't. Her man was missing her. With a smile on her face, she decided that she'd drive to Virginia and surprise him. As soon as her last class ended on Friday, she'd hop on the highway. It was only a three-hour drive. Reign was going to get her man.

Chapter Fifteen

J ules sat on his couch with a menacing glare on his face. Lyric had been gone for more than six hours, and she wasn't answering her phone. Jules didn't know where to begin looking for her, and he was mad enough to spit nails. He was trying hard not to judge her, but Lyric had him fucked up. He didn't want to make Bella aware that anything was out of the ordinary, so he took her out to eat and they spent some father daughter time. She was under the impression that her mother was booked for the day doing hair. Once they got back to the house, she went into her room to get on the phone, play the game, or whatever teenagers do, and Jules tried to calm himself with a blunt. The weed didn't do anything to ease Jules' fears or calm his frazzled nerves. Now, he knew how she must have felt when he was wildin' out sniffing coke. His father dying did something to him. Jules had never felt a pain so deep or a burden so heavy. All the running the streets, killing people, losing his dad, it all came crashing down on him, and the only solace he found was when he sniffed coke.

The coke fucked with his mood something terrible though, and it turned Jules into a completely different person. Lyric rode with him the entire time though, and he was determined to do that for her, but the shit she was doing, he wasn't going to tolerate. When the front door finally opened, it was almost 9 p.m. Jules glared at Lyric as she entered the living room with a sheepish look on her face. He could tell she'd found what she was looking for, because no longer was she anxious, tense, or defensive. Her face was soft, and her eyes were full of regret. She was only apologetic to him though because she was high and content. Jules knew what it was, and it pissed him off.

She took timid steps towards the couch, and the face that normally made his heart smile, had his blood boiling. "Where the fuck you been? And I suggest that you not lie," Jules all but growled.

Lyric sighed. Most of the time, she could get her way with Jules, but she knew she'd messed up big time. He was already heated, so lying would do nothing for the situation. He was too smart to try and fool anyway. Now that he knew she had a habit, he was going to be on her like white on rice. With the pill she had in her system though, Lyric was calm enough to try and reason with him. Sitting down beside him, she chose to tell the truth.

"I went to my mom's house and got some of the pills that she had left over from her knee surgery. She doesn't take them like that."

Jules sucked his teeth. After calling Jason and her doctor, he didn't even think to call Lyric's mother. It was as if she read his mind. "Jules, please don't worry my mother with this. I'm going to stop, okay. It's hard to stop cold turkey, and I know you know that."

Not wanting to argue, he chose his words very carefully. "It's not going to be easy to quit, and I know you know that. You just gon' have to do it, and I'm not here for all the excuses, ma. I'm really not, 'cause I know you know me better than to think I'm gon' sit back and watch you pop pills every day. You can't even function without them shits, and that's a real live problem. I'm going to let Bella stay with a friend this weekend, and you gon' get right, ma. That's not a got damn request either."

Lyric saw the fire blazing in her husband's eyes, and she knew he meant business. There was nothing she could say, so she just went upstairs and took a shower. Lyric wasn't looking forward to the process of quitting the pills because of how harsh the withdrawal symptoms were, but when Jules put his foot down, she was smart enough to know there was no getting around it. Still, Lyric removed two pills from the inside of her bra that were wrapped in aluminum foil. Looking over her shoulder to make sure the coast was clear, she entered her huge walk-in closet, and pulled a shoe box from the bottom of a stack. Lyric removed the lid and stuffed the pills inside one of her sneakers. No matter what Jules said, she was going to keep a stash for a rainy day.

"I'm just gon' keep it real with you, shawty. My girl is coming, and if you come to the party, you gon' have to act like you don't know me like that," Tre told Venisha.

She raised one eyebrow and looked at him like he was crazy. The nigga had just invited her to the party a day ago. She knew there was a female that was at a lot of his shows and on his Instagram page, but Venisha wasn't shocked when he invited her to the party. Shit, all rappers, athletes, dope boys, regular niggas, were dogs.

"Okayyyyy..." Her voice trailed off. "So, I can come, but I have to act like I don't know you."

Tre met Venisha at the barber shop. His barber had a few celebrity clients, and he even traveled places to cut their hair. Tre started going to him, and after his first cut with the man, he refused to go anywhere else. Venisha was actually his barber's cousin. She cut hair too and ran the shop when he traveled. Tre flirted with her here and there, but they had never had sex. Tired of being a good boy, he decided to have her on standby until Reign called him and let him know that she was on her way in town.

"Yeah, I mean, that's a problem?"

Venisha sucked her teeth and shook her head. "No, it's not a problem."

Tre smiled and exited the barber shop. That was the reason why he got so agitated when Reign didn't jump for him. No matter what he said or did, no other female challenged him or denied him. Reign was his first choice though, so when she told him that she could make his party, he had no problem dropping Venisha. She was local, so maybe they'd end up getting together one day. It just wouldn't be at his party.

Tre wanted to show Reign that he was all in, so he went and bought a toothbrush, some girly lotion and perfume, socks, hair products, makeup remover and all that shit for her to have at his place. He wanted her to be able to come to him at the drop of a dime and not even have to worry about packing a bag. Tre went to the mall and got Reign ten outfits and five pairs of shoes. The clothes ranged from leggings and shit by PINK to club dresses, jeans, and shirts. The shoes consisted of two pair of Louboutin's, a pair of Jordan's, some Gucci slides, and some Gucci sneakers. Tre left everything in the bags so she wouldn't trip thinking the shit belonged to some other female. Tre was giving Reign until the summer, and that was it. He admired the fact that she didn't want to quit school, but once the year was done, she better be ready to make major moves, or he was going to have to be done with her. She was gorgeous, and the pussy was good. Tre wanted her there beside him every day, not just weekends.

By the time he got back home, Reign was pulling up in his driveway, and he waited for her to get out of the car before rushing over to her and picking her up. Tre hugged her tight and spun her around causing her to squeal. "My baby came to her nigga. That's what the fuck I'm talkin' 'bout," he replied before placing her feet down on the ground. Tre leaned forward and placed a juicy kiss on Reign's lips. He hadn't seen her in over a week, and he was ready to fuck.

After he gave her a tour of the house, and she put all of the things he bought her away, Reign and Tre had mind blowing sex. They took a shower together and then got dressed. Since it was a house party, Reign wanted to be chill, so she dressed comfortably in a white Gucci tee that she wore as a dress and the slides that Tre bought her. She kept her make-up light and natural looking, but she was still killing 'em. Tre dressed in white Belstaff jeans, a red Gucci shirt, and Gucci sneakers. Three chains hung from his neck, and his Rolex was blinging. Tre looked hood rich as fuck, and Reign complimented the fuck out of him. No longer shying away from the attention, she made numerous snaps of his home, and him and her. They were flexing heavy showing off their grills and all of their jewelry. Reign posted her gifts as well. The doorbell rang, and she kept flexing as Tre let Choppa and a few more guys in.

He took Reign by surprise, when he grabbed her phone from her hand and got on her Snapchat. "Yeah, this Tre da muhfuckin' Don, and all y'all lil' weak ass niggas in my girl DM's on some sucka shit. Shawty is mine. She ain't got no conversation for you bastards."

Reign laughed as he handed her back the phone and went to holla at his niggas. She wished Jayla had come. Within thirty minutes, the house was filled with more than fifty people, and Reign didn't know half of them. Tre was smoking, drinking, and having a good time. Reign was turning up too, but it would have been more fun if Jayla was there. She knew she couldn't expect her cousin to drop everything she had going on and come with her every time she wanted to see Tre. He was her dude now, so she had to put on her big girl panties and come alone. Reign hadn't seen Tre in about fifteen minutes. She was sipping henny and texting Jayla. The sudden urge to pee hit her, and Reign went to the bathroom. While she was sitting on the toilet, the room suddenly began to spin. Reaching out, Reign held onto the wall and closed her eyes. She hit the blunt a few times and had less than two shots of henny. No way should she be feeling like she was on a merry-go-round. She had to find Tre. Reign wiped herself and stood up. "Fuck," she hissed after she wobbled and fell against the wall.

Something was wrong. She didn't feel right. Reign concentrated as hard as she could to wash her hands and get herself out of the bathroom. She had to find Tre. As soon as she opened the bathroom door, she walked right into a short dark-skinned nigga with gold fronts. "Damn, lil' mama you good?" he asked.

Tears filled Reign's eyes. She was fucked up, and she knew what she was feeling wasn't normal. She'd been drugged. Her tongue felt thick, and her words slurred. "No, I need to find Tre." She cried.

"Aight. Come on." The guy gently pulled her arm and guided her, but Reign quickly saw that he was guiding her to a bedroom.

"I don't want to lay down. I need Tre." She could barely keep her eyes open. Reign didn't even realize that old dude was locking the door, as she called Tre since her phone was in her hand.

His phone rang a few times before he came over to her and took it from her hand. "No, you don't need the phone, baby girl. I got what you need."

"Huh?" Reign looked up confused and had to squint her eyes because she was seeing double. Before she could grasp the concept of what was happening, he pushed her back on the bed and got on top of her.

Reign's arms felt heavy as lead and she was trying her best to push him, but she wasn't moving him in the least. "Nooooooo!" she screamed at the top of her lungs, but it didn't matter. The music was so loud that no one would hear her.

"Please get off of me. No!" she cried as she beat him in the chest with her fist and he scratched up her thigh trying to get her panties off.

Outside in his car, Tre licked his lips as he looked anxiously over at Venisha. "You gotta hurry up 'cause shorty gon' be looking for me in a minute."

He had no intentions of fucking her that night, but she came to his party half naked, gone off a pill, and ready to do all kinds of nasty shit to him. He'd popped a pill as well and after she cornered him and begged to suck his dick, he snuck out to the car for a quickie.

A wicked grin spread across Venisha's face. "Oh, I can do that for sure."

He helped her out by freeing his dick from the confinement of his boxers. Venisha wasted no time taking him into her mouth and slurping on him like ice cream on a hot day. "Damn, baby," he moaned as she deep throated him.

His phone rung and Tre blew out a shaky breath. What Venisha was doing to him felt so damn good. He started not to answer for Reign, but he knew she would only keep calling. He was going to shoot her a lie that he had to run to the store.

"Please get off of me. No!" Tre's face crumpled as he heard Reign screaming and crying. He was confused, but there was no mistaking the panic and fear in her voice.

"Move," he stated, pushing Venisha's head back damn near snapping her neck.

Tre stuffed his dick back inside his boxers, fixed his jeans, and jumped out of his car. He had hella bedrooms, and he had no idea which one Reign was in. He knew good and got damn well a nigga wasn't violating his shorty in his crib. Tre burst through his front door, and the party was so lit that no one even paid him any attention. Tre rushed to the guest bedroom downstairs, and he was glad he made that his first stop. When he twisted the knob, the door was locked, and he began to beat on it. His house was made out of the finest materials. He knew he wouldn't be able to kick the damn door in. After he beat on the door for a good minute with no answer, he was tempted to try kicking it in, but before he could lift his foot, the door flew open. On the other side of it stood Choppa's cousin. The fuck nigga was sweating and breathing hard.

Tre's eyes flew over to the bed and his heart fell into his stomach when he saw Reign on the bed crying hysterically. "Fuck did you do?" he screeched before punching the man in the face, causing him to stumble back a few feet.

"Nigga, I thought the bitches at this party was for everybody. Shit, you was in the car with old girl. How was I supposed to know—" before he could complete his sentence, Tre was on his ass. He punched the man over and over again for a good two minutes, before he felt himself being pulled off the barely conscious man. His face was beaten to a bloody pulp.

"What the fuck, Tre?" Choppa asked with wide eyes.

The music had stopped, and all eyes were on Tre. "This what niggas do? I let bastards in my home, and y'all raping females? Get the fuck out!" he roared so loud that those standing closest to him jumped.

No one knew exactly what was going on, but they could see that Tre wasn't playing. Everyone left the house. Choppa's cousin couldn't even walk out, he had to be carried out. Once everyone was gone, Tre frantically searched the house for Reign. "Reign!" he screamed searching every single room to no avail. He finally decided to check outside, and her car was gone. Tre flopped down on the couch and put his head in his hands. He fucked up. He fucked up bad.

Reign cried for an entire hour. Her mind was still foggy, so she went and parked her car down the street to call 9-1-1. She was coherent enough to know that she had been drugged and raped in the home of her boyfriend. For as fucked up as she was, she heard the guy that raped her say something about Tre being in the car with a girl. All she could think the entire time was that her dad was right. She was in an unfamiliar city with a nigga that obviously didn't give two fucks about her, and she'd been hurt in his care. When the EMT's arrived, aside from saying she'd been drugged and raped, Reign shut down. All she could do was cry as they put her on a gurney and in the back of the ambulance. She didn't speak for the entire hospital ride, until they asked if there was someone they call for her. Reign simply nodded her head. "Yes, my father."

When Reign came to, she had a pounding headache. Before she

even opened her eyes, the throbbing in her head made her groan. When she did open her eyes, the brightness of the room hurt her eyes, causing her to squint. Reign noticed that she was in a hospital bed, and when she turned to her left, she saw her father and her mother. Jules' jaws were tight. The look in his eyes scared her. He was out for blood, and Reign had to concentrate hard to think about what had happened. The throbbing between her legs quickly jogged her memory. When she turned her head, and her parents saw that she was awake, her mother rushed over to the bed while Jules remained seated.

"Oh my God, Reign. You don't know how scared I've been," her mother stated. Lyric's eyes were glossy from the tears that swam in them.

"How long have I been asleep?" she asked in a timid voice.

"We just got here an hour ago. I don't know babe. We got the initial call three hours ago. The doctor did confirm that you had a very small dose of Rophypnol in your system. Someone absolutely drugged you. I just thank God that it wasn't enough to make you unaware of what was going on." A fat tear spilled over Lyric's eyelid.

Reign's eyes darted over to her father. She already knew what was about to go down. He stood up and came over to the bed. "I need you to tell me everything that happened. I mean everything," he stated in a no-nonsense tone. "The police will be back up here to talk to you, but you already know what it is. Don't tell them pigs nothing. I'll handle everything."

Had Reign been in her right mind, she wouldn't have called her father. She was high out her mind, and she just needed someone that had her best interest in heart. Now that she was sober, Reign feared what was going to happen, but there was nothing she could do to take it back. So, she told her father everything that she remembered.

Chapter Sixteen

"When are we going home?" Reign asked her mother confused. She'd been released from the hospital ten hours prior, and her father had gotten a hotel suite for her, him, and Reign.

They'd been in the hotel room for four hours, and Reign just wanted to go home. Before Lyric could answer her question, Jules entered the hotel room. "Reign get dressed and come with me."

She knew better than to ask any questions, so she got up and threw on some clothes. Reign then followed her father to the elevator and stayed quiet as he pressed buttons. Reign's phone had been blowing up, but she hadn't even been looking to see who was calling or texting her. Her feelings were beyond hurt. She'd really been feeling Tre, and although he wasn't the one to bring direct harm to her, the shit still hurt. How do you get raped at your nigga's crib while he's there? Reign was embarrassed, and she felt dirty. Not even soaking in the tub made her feel better. She'd been screened for STD's and given antibiotics, but what if she woke up in a week with blisters on her pussy? You had to be a nasty muhfucka to rape someone. Reign refused to assume that her rapist's health was up to par.

She knew her dad was pissed, so she chose not to talk. After they got in his car and had been riding for about five minutes, her stomach began to churn. He wasn't going to leave Virginia without fucking Tre up. Reign wasn't sure why she hadn't thought of it earlier, but that's just how her dad got down. He didn't want her talking to cops because he was going to handle it, and there were a bunch of different things wrong with that scenario. First of all, Tre was famous. If Jules did something to him and got arrested, Reign's world would be over. She loved her father so much, and she didn't want him getting in any trouble behind her.

Secondly, some may call her dumb, but she didn't want Tre hurt. Reign had no plans of ever dealing with him again, but that didn't mean she wanted him dead. It felt as if her throat were closing up, and her hands began to tremble as they pulled up in Tre's driveway. "Dad please. I don't want to be here," she told Jules with a shaky voice.

Ignoring her, he pulled a 9mm from underneath his seat and emerged from the car. "Come on," he demanded as Reign took in the cars in the driveway.

Her uncles Jacques was there. This shit was about to end bad as hell. Tears burned her eyes as she exited the car. She should have never called her father. She would almost rather the police handle the shit. Being apart of a crime family was weird as fuck. Reign followed her father up to the door, and a low whimper escaped her lips when he entered the house without knocking or ringing the doorbell. Reign gasped as the entered the living room and she saw Jacques, J.J., and J2 standing in the middle of the room with a beaten and bloody Tre on the floor. The man that raped her was beside him. Tre looked up at Reign, and he looked so pitiful that she had to look away. "Reign, I'm sorry. I swear, I only left the house for five minutes. I didn't know this would happen," he cried. His left eye was swollen shut, and his lip was busted.

"Shut the fuck up nigga." J2 barked. "My sister came here to be with you, and you let your low life ass friends rape her? Sounds like a fuck nigga to me." J2 was equally as pissed as his father was. All of them were. J.J. and Jacques were ready to murk niggas.

"I didn't know he would do no shit like that. He's not even my friend. He was a friend of a friend." The tough guy persona that Tre had in his raps was gone. Despite what had happened to her, Reign felt bad for him.

"Dad please let's just go," she begged Jules. "He really didn't know what was going down. We were separated for a while. I was on my phone while he mingled and entertained his guest. I guess this creep slipped something in my drink and took it from there." It hurt her that Tre was with another female while she was being violated, but he didn't deserve to die for it.

Jules was agitated that Reign was taking up for Tre. "Baby Girl, I know you not that gone over this wack ass gangsta rapper. You really defending him?" Jules' finger caressed the trigger of his gun.

"Dad, I will never deal with him again. But please don't harm him. He's famous, and he's not worth it. Please let's just go."

Jules kissed his teeth. He gave no fucks about the nigga being famous. Anybody could get it. Anybody. Reign was soft, but that was cool. Jules had enough gangsta in him for the both of them. With a sadistic smile on his face, he raised his gun and pulled the trigger as Reign's hands flew over her mouth to conceal the screams.

Note From The Author

I hadn't planned on doing another Baptiste Boys story. Out of all the books that I have written, the Baptiste Boys series are a favorite among my readers, and I felt that I stretched it for as long as I could. Most of you guys hated In Love With a Trap God because you said I didn't give Kymani closure. Y'all killed me in the reviews, and I was ready to quit writing lol. But people have been asking and asking, and I hope I delivered. However, after this series, the Baptiste Boys will rest. I wasn't sure of how they would be perceived, and I am elated that they are the guys that gained me tons of new readers. I still get asked about that series two years later.

ABOUT THE AUTHOR

Natisha Raynor discovered her love for reading in third grade. As she got older she preferred being in her bedroom reading a good book versus playing outside. Natisha began writing her own stories at 12 years old, when the books she was reading no longer held her interest. Natisha wrote for fun for many years until she reached her mid-twenties and sought out a publishing deal. In 2015 she self-published her first novel and since then she's penned more than thirty books. Natisha resides in Raleigh, North Carolina with her two teenaged children.

facebook.com/Natisha-Raynor-Presents-1003152116362757

instagram.com/author_natisha_raynor

ALSO BY NATISHA RAYNOR

If you haven't checked out other books by me, I have a very lengthy catalog.
The titles that I have under Royalty are:

Idris and Wisdom: The Most Savage Summer Ever (3 Book Series)

Cherished By A Thug (2 Book Series)

Shawty Got A Thang For Them Country Boys (3 Book Series)

STAY CONNECTED

Please join my Facebook Group:

My Heart Beats Books

My Facebook like page is:

Author Natisha Raynor

Royalty Publishing House is now accepting manuscripts from aspiring or experienced urban romance authors!

WHAT MAY PLACE YOU ABOVE THE REST:

Heroes who are the ultimate book bae: strong-willed, maybe a little rough around the edges but willing to risk it all for the woman he loves.

Heroines who are the ultimate match: the girl next door type, not perfect - has her faults but is still a decent person. One who is willing to risk it all for the man she loves.

The rest is up to you! Just be creative, think out of the box, keep it sexy and intriguing!

If you'd like to join the Royal family, send us the first 15K words (60 pages) of your completed manuscript to submissions@royaltypublishinghouse.com

LIKE OUR PAGE!

Be sure to <u>LIKE</u> our Royalty Publishing House page on Facebook!

CPSIA information can be obtained
at www.ICGtesting.com
Printed in the USA
LVHW04s2339191018
594246LV00001B/109/P

9 781726 836302